THE WAY

Ossie heard whispers pass throu___ ___
*rat?" "Ain't got a clue." "Who's ___ ___
hear."* It was a thing swamp folk said, *Fern Chui*. It meant an
orphan, as they were often found hiding among sheltering ferns.

Another time they passed a black bear halfway up a fiddle-
wood tree. "How you doin, Brother Bear?" said the gator.

"Doin good, Will," the bear called. Then he added, "S'pose
you know there's a rat on your back?"

"Sure he knows, Bear!" said Preacher. "How's he gonna
not know!?"

"Only commentin on it," the bear replied.

"The boy's named Ossie," Will said as they drifted on, and
the bear said, "Nice to meet you, Ossie."

And the little rat nodded to him.

Preacher said, "Ossie's not much for talkin."

That's the way it went and the days had no end to them.
Ossie and the alligator were quietly crossing the swamp when
the little rat saw something move on a near shore. Was it her?
It moved from the leafy shadow and wasn't a rat at all, but a
mother possum, foraging food, babies clinging all over. Uncle
Will said, "You want to go over? You want to say hello?"

Ossie shook his head no. Will let it go at that. He knew
the swamp rat might never go over, might never say hello.

But change, Will knew, would have to come from Ossie.

"The writing is uncommonly evocative, and this is the kind of
folkloric fiction that kids can treasure."   —*Booklist*

"Echoes of both *The Wind in the Willows* and *The Jungle
Book*....Readers may enjoy Crocker's low-key brand of humor
and non-preachy philosophizing."   —*Kirkus Reviews*

OTHER BOOKS YOU MAY ENJOY

THE TALE OF THE
SWAMP RAT

Carter Crocker

illustrated by the author

PUFFIN BOOKS

To Emily Heath,

the editor, without whom it would not have been

PUFFIN BOOKS
Published by the Penguin Group
Penguin Young Readers Group, 345 Hudson Street, New York, New York 10014, U.S.A.
Penguin Group (Canada), 10 Alcorn Avenue, Toronto, Ontario, Canada M4V 3B2
(a division of Pearson Penguin Canada Inc.)
Penguin Books Ltd, 80 Strand, London WC2R 0RL, England
Penguin Ireland, 25 St Stephen's Green, Dublin 2, Ireland (a division of Penguin Books Ltd)
Penguin Group (Australia), 250 Camberwell Road, Camberwell, Victoria 3124, Australia
(a division of Pearson Australia Group Pty Ltd)
Penguin Books India Pvt Ltd, 11 Community Centre,
Panchsheel Park, New Delhi - 110 017, India
Penguin Group (NZ), Cnr Airborne and Rosedale Roads, Albany, Auckland,
New Zealand (a division of Pearson New Zealand Ltd)
Penguin Books (South Africa) (Pty) Ltd, 24 Sturdee Avenue,
Rosebank, Johannesburg 2196, South Africa

Registered Offices: Penguin Books Ltd, 80 Strand, London WC2R 0RL, England

First published in the United States of America by Philomel Books,
a division of Penguin Young Readers Group, 2003
Published by Puffin Books, a division of Penguin Young Readers Group, 2005

1 3 5 7 9 10 8 6 4 2

Copyright © Carter Crocker, 2003
All rights reserved

THE LIBRARY OF CONGRESS HAS CATALOGED THE PHILOMEL EDITION AS FOLLOWS:
Crocker, Carter.
The tale of the swamp rat / by Carter Crocker.
p. cm.
Summary: Guided by an ancient alligator, a silent young rat learns to find
his own way in the drought-stricken swamp, despite having been orphaned
under circumstances that sometimes cause other animals to reject him.
ISBN: 0-399-23964-2 (hc)
[1. Rats—Fiction. 2. Swamp animals—Fiction. 3. Coming of age—Fiction.
4. Orphans—Fiction. 5. Droughts—Fiction. 6. Swamp ecology—Fiction.
7. Ecology—Fiction. 8. Florida—Fiction.] I. Title.
PZ7.C86968Tal 2003
[Fic]—dc21 2003000429

Puffin Books ISBN 0-14-240314-8

Printed in the United States of America

THE TALE OF THE
SWAMP RAT

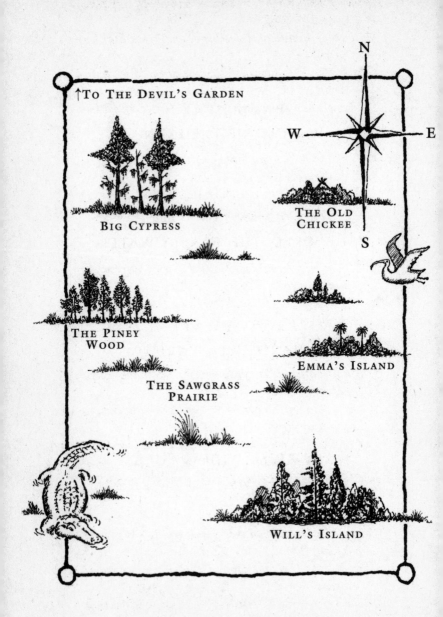

↑To The Devil's Garden

N
W   E
S

BIG CYPRESS

THE OLD CHICKEE

THE PINEY WOOD

EMMA'S ISLAND

THE SAWGRASS PRAIRIE

WILL'S ISLAND

The old Marsh Rabbit, by force of bad habit, was dinin
       on pickerelweed,
when out of the shroud of a wintry cloud, comes Hawk at
       lightnin speed.
"Oh, I'm done!" cries the Rabbit, "my world is come to
       ruin!"
But Hawk, he only smiles and says, "Friend, tell me how
       you doin."
"Say whaaat?" says Rabbit. "Just hold on, son!
Did you not eat my fambly one by one?
You subtract ever time we multiply,
so you gotta lotta nerve, askin how am I!"
"That's true," says Hawk, "but I think we should try to
       let those bygones be goin on by."

And off to the East, dead and deceased, Possum lays
       under an oak,
when Panther appears and looks and sneers, "Brother,
       enough of the joke.
I know you're alive, I saw how you blinked,
so why do you lay there and play you're extinct?"
"I'll answer you that, you old devil-cat!" the pitiful
       Possum squeals:
"Cause I find it nerve-wrackin to see that you're snackin
       between your regular meals!"
Says Panther, "No cryin, I'm not here denyin I feasted on
       kith and your kin,
But I won't eat a bite before supper tonight, so can't we
       be civil till then?"

The multitudes will end their feuds and be like birds of
       a feather,
when the lone Lost One comes along and brings em all
       together.
                —from "The Song of the Swamp"

WHERE WE ARE AND WHO I AM

To start with, this is all true. I'm almost certain of that. What happened, happened here in the Great Swamp, a place as wide as the world. If you were a drop of water, it would take you a year to move from one end to the other. It's as big as that, or that's what I've been told.

Our swamp is a muddle of marsh and forest and water and land and everything else. There are broad wet fields of grass. There are small clumps of land, round and thick and wild with trees. There is open water. There are low islands, stretching long and thin. The water is shallow, most places, most times. A leggy bird could wade the whole swamp, or that's what I've been told and I choose to believe it. Just beside us is a place of Big Cypress and farther on the land turns dry and hard. There's nothing of account beyond that.

Everything lives in our swamp. There are large things, small things, things flying, crawling, swimming, friendly, not, tall, short, right, wrong, plant, animal, and one snake unlike any other. They live, they die, they matter, they don't. This is a big place, or did I say that?

Pahayokee, the Indians have called it. The grassy water. Home is what I call it. And this is where it happened.

I won't claim I saw every bit of what happened, start to finish. Some of it I heard from the birds. Birds always tell me things. Birds like me and trust me. *Here is how it is, Little Mole*, they say. *Go tell the others, Little Mole*. I say, Of course. Of course I will. They know I'll get it right.

That is how I tell you this story now.

PART ONE

A CHILD OF THE FERN

CHAPTER 1
A PLACE TO START

Change always comes on a Wind;
good, bad, or indifferent, it comes on a Wind.
—a swamp saying

When the whole thing began, it was dark. It was as dark as it's ever been or ever will be. Not a moon, not a star, not the blink of a firefly to light that smothering night. That's how it was when it all began.

And out in a sawgrass prairie, on a small island, there was a flustered heap of twigs called a lodge. A Rat-Father crawled from his home, into a night soggy with orchid-scent. He nosed the ground, for grubs, for bugs, busily digging the soft soil.

And then, he stopped.

He stayed there, where he was, not moving the least little bit. Something wasn't right in the forest. He didn't know what—but he knew something was wrong. He smelled the night air and smelled no danger. He listened and heard only quiet.

Suddenly he felt how still the darkness was around him. He had never known the forest to be so dark and so still, and it puzzled him. Something was not right. He sensed that some change was somehow coming in the swamp. But he did not, could not know what sort of change it was.

The Rat-Father moved on, in that careful, watchful way small animals have.

Now, sooner or later the sun was going to rise. And sooner or later it did, at first a milky glow beyond the trees, a slow dim dawning. And in the gloom the small rat didn't see a shadow move within a shadow, high in a dark tree.

In a quiet flashing of wings, an owl slid from the branches and down to the swamp rat.

The Rat-Father heard a rustling of feathers, and jumped to hide among cypress roots. Sharp claws cut the air just over him. The owl dove at him once more and the rat raced across the swamp forest floor. The bird lunged again, and again the Rat-Father darted away. He leaped for the safety of thick-grown grasses. There were feathers filling the air now and the owl had worked itself into a fury! But he could not reach the Rat-Father.

By the time the owl had flown back to the tree, the rat was back safe in the lodge. He could hear the old bird far off among the trees, hollering at him and the world in general, "D'you think I care!? Only a measly little rat! Wouldn't have held me till lunch! D'you think I care!?"

The Rat-Father huddled in the twig-nest for some long

time and as he sat, he worried for his children. He worried over one more than the rest. . . .

It was light before long, a day in early Spring, slow moving and heavy with heat. There were gray-bellied clouds to the east, but none with good rain. There hadn't been much rain the season before and the swamp was going dry. Even rats could walk long stretches of it.

A black snake glided across a small pool, smooth and wordless. An alligator bellowed in the far somewhere, a long-off sound and pleasant. Two yellow butterflies, pale as that morning sun, passed in fidgeting flight. The nesting trees were full of ibis and egret. Dragonflies danced to dragonfly music.

For the swamp rat called Ossie, it was his third week in the world.

He was born one of twelve and it was he that his father worried over. Ossie was small, much smaller than the rest, and skinny as the reeds. A runt is what he was. A pitiful runt. He was shy and unsure and quiet. He was very quiet. Within a week, his brothers and sisters were chattering without pause, yet Ossie had not spoken a word, not made a sound. The Rat-Father and Rat-Mother wondered if he ever might.

Did Ossie have a voice? Who could say? He was shy. The simple thought of sound tangled in his throat and made him ashamed and made him not try. Did Ossie have a voice? Even he didn't know. That's how shy he was.

When the swamp rats were out of the lodge that Spring day, they played and played hard. They ran, they chased, they hid, they sought, they fought, they laughed. Except Ossie. He stood, he watched. Quiet.

The Rat-Father saw and he wondered about this odd child, silent, alone, born to a Time of Drought. What would the Prophet say?

I should explain about the Prophet, an old Ironhead Stork. This bird, it was said, had great powers. This bird, it was said, could understand omens and read signs. He was called Bubba. He lived on an island many miles off; but he moved from place to place, explaining the truth and revealing mysteries. Folk brought fish in trade for his prophecies and Bubba brought peace to their troubled minds.

Bubba was a big bird, body of white, pure and clean, but his neck and head were dark, wrinkled, and without feather. His eyes were bottomless black; you could not look away from them. Wherever he went, folk looked and listened and he liked that.

"Listen to me!" he would shout, and folk would listen.

(I must also tell you that I have known many Ironhead Storks in my day and they've been good friends, every one. They are fine birds, majestic in their way. They are loyal folk and decent, through and through. But Bubba, he was something altogether else.)

Once way back, when the Rat-Father was young, the Prophet Bubba had come to this island. Someone had found strange tracks in a clearing. Someone had called for Bubba.

The tracks formed a giant pattern, a circle in a circle, on and on, like rippling rings in the water. The Prophet understood. It meant disease would visit this place. It would come in four weeks, same as there were four circles. It would stay on the island four months. Each family would lose four of its own.

The only hope, he said, was to ring the island with tamarind leaves, laid five deep.

They worked together, side by side. Birds pulled leaves from branches and brought them to rats, who carried them to the island's edge where raccoon, possum, and mice made a giant circle.

They waited. Days passed into weeks. Four months came and four months went. There was celebration then. No disease had found its way onto the island. Bubba's magic had worked.

Now, the Rat-Father knew he'd made those tracks himself, late in the night, when a sick stomach kept him from sleeping. He had gone out in the dark, wandering in half-dreaming circles, till he burped a foul burp and the ache was gone from his gut.

But folk believed the Prophet. And who was he, this one little rat, to say they were wrong, all of them wrong?

What would the Prophet have to say about Ossie, he wondered.

In time the Rat-Father called the children in and led them into the forest. He was going to teach them the ways of the swamp, he said. He would show them how to find food and not become it. They moved across the small island, turning leaves, digging the spongy soil for grubs.

But Ossie's mind soon drifted from this. There was too much else to see here: trees, vines, flowers, all of them incredible; the sky, a bottomless blue; and the air, beautiful to smell.

This was an exceptional world and he wanted to see more. The silent little rat moved past a giant fern and a field of silk grass, past a tree dying in a slow embrace of the Strangler Fig.

He saw it all with dreamer-eyes and touched each thing to make it real.

He ate a berry that was half gone bad and the taste stayed with him all day. He climbed the side of a cabbage palm and fell and knocked the wind out of himself. He scared a twig-skinny lizard and its half-dozen young ones, babies as tiny as blackberry leaves. Overhead wide flocks of egrets passed and songbirds were everywhere.

Around him, below him, there was a small and less-seen world. Hidden among the grasses and folds of leaves, there were bugs and tiny frogs no bigger than bugs. From them came a chorus of countless voices, melting to one, *skree-skree-skreeee,* ratcheting, rising, falling. It was a never-ending noise, like some grand machine that made the whole swamp run.

An exceptional world is what this was.

Ossie had wandered off the island, out where the water had been, with no thought to where he was or where he was going.

CHAPTER 2
FINDING A WAY

He walked the dried muck until he reached a deep channel, still full. The water was smooth, a perfect mirror. Ossie leaned and looked and saw himself and behind him there rose a great forest, a whole full world, the upside-down of his.

He turned. A gray cypress grew from the water here and around its trunk were gnarled knobby knees. As he hopped onto one, he began to hear a low rushing. The sound was new to him and strange, but soon he understood. . . .

It was wind, a long slow wind, making its way across the swamp. He listened, carefully, as if it were sharing some secret with him. The warm wind brought a smell of sawgrass and water, trees and sky, plant and animal, yesterday and tomorrow, and everything in between.

And then, in another blinking of an eye, the wind whipped

on and with it came butterflies. And more butterflies, more and more, thousands upon thousands, more than Ossie could dream. The sun dappled through them as it did through cypress leaves. They were the same color, but each caught the light a different way and they were every color. Their wings beat the air, a million pair, but made no noise. They were going somewhere, for some reason, and he heard their tiny insect voices. *"Will it be better there?" "How much farther?" "Are we there yet?"*

He sat and watched as they passed and he wondered, *Where are they going? What place are they looking for? How could it be better than this?* Then he noticed something across the water, on another island, only a few dozen feet off. He wasn't sure what it was. Until, through the butterfly-cloud, he saw. It was a rat like himself.

Or not like himself. It was a girl-rat, about his age he guessed. She saw him across the water. She smiled. He smiled. He wanted to say something, but couldn't. Then every butterfly was gone, as if they'd never been. The girl was still there. Only she and Ossie had seen them, had shared them. Then she disappeared in thick plants and he was alone.

Ossie hopped to a taller cypress knee and the next. But he never got to a place where he could see her again. He saw a homely armadillo rooting around the loose soil. But no girl.

He wondered if he dreamed it, the whole thing, the girl, the butterflies and all. He didn't notice a couple of wasps hovering around his head.

"Little Rat," said one, "what you doin?"

Ossie said nothing and was embarrassed to hear it.

"What you lookin to find?" the wasp went on.

Ossie hopped down the cypress knees, back onto land.

"I'm Tim," said the other, "this is Tom. We're brothers."

"And have been," the first one said, "since we was infants."

"Who would you be?"

There was no answer.

"I'm thinkin," the second wasp said, "this fella's not a big talker."

They floated over him, lazy legs dangling, and he watched.

"You in there?" said one.

"Helloooo-oooo-ooo!"

"Anybody home . . . ?"

"What's the matter with the Little Rat?" said the other.

"I believe he don't like us," said the first.

But of course he liked them. He had no reason not to. The wasps gave up and flew off.

Ossie went after them and lost them once and saw them again by an old inkwood tree, where the ground was woven over with fallen branches. He struggled over limbs, one after another, and at last caught up with them in a clear flat spot.

The second one saw him first. "LookoutTomarat!" "WhereTimwhereisit?"

Maybe, Ossie thought, he'd found a couple of different wasps, different wasps named Tim and Tom.

But there was something he didn't know. And it was this. A wasp has two moods. And that's all. They're either pleasant and curious, eager to know every last thing about you. Or they're crazy mean bullies. There's no middle with wasps.

"What you doin there?" one hissed. "Why you sneakin up on us?" the other spat.

Ossie stepped back, but the wasps flew at him. They flew tight circles around him, tighter and tighter, knocking into him. There was nowhere to run.

"I'm thinkin," one was saying, "Little Rat don't know what it is to get the sting of a wasp!"

"Two wasps!" the other yelled. "How you like the sound of them apples, huh?"

Ossie was even more quiet than he had been.

"My brother axed you a question, why don't you answer!" the first one screamed.

"Why don't you answer my brother why you don't answer!" the second one screamed.

Ossie had no answer.

"How come he won't say nothin, Tom?"

"I'll tell you how come, Tim! He's a high and mighty little snob, that's how come!"

"That's how come?" Tim hollered at Ossie. "You think you're better than us!?"

They flew around and around him, jabbing their stingers closer and closer to him.

"Forget them," from still another voice. It was under Ossie's feet. It was the voice of a mole, a cousin of mine. He pushed from the damp soil. "They're nothin but talk."

"Who asked you?" asked Tim.

"Yeah, who?" asked Tom.

"They won't sting you just to prove a point," my cousin told Ossie. "Even a wasp isn't that ignerunt."

"Says who!" said Tim.

"That's what you think!" said Tom.

"They get one sting and they die," the mole went on, "so

the last thing they're goin to do is sting you. I mean it. The Last Thing."

The wasps lost their tempers then. "Lousy mole! Let me at him, Tim, just let me at him!" the first one screamed.

But the mole only laughed. He called out, small, defiant, "Let the mangroves take you!"

Now that, in this swamp, is a very serious thing to say. No wasp could let a mole talk to him that way. A mole had to pay for saying a thing like that. They flew at my cousin and he slipped back in the earth.

The wasps crawled over the ground, cursing him, trying to find him.

"Ow, Tom!" said one.

"Ow what, Tim?" the other asked.

"You stung me, you MOron!"

"Who you callin MOron, you MOron!" yelled Tom.

"Takes a MOron to know a MOron!" yelled Tim. "And I'll prove it! I'll sting you right back! So there!"

There was silence. It was sinking in on them, what they'd done that they shouldn't have. Ossie moved quickly off. And two wasps with bad tempers chased each other out over the dry grasses and dropped into the swamp channel, where they went floating toward the mangroves, quiet, lifeless, morons.

He had meant to find his family after that, but Ossie found himself thinking of the girl-rat. It was odd, how she stuck in his thoughts. He hadn't met her, only glimpsed her. He didn't know anything about her, only that she was exceptional, re-markable, amazing, full of something like light, the only one of her there was. It wasn't fair to have seen her so quickly. Not fair at all.

Ossie wandered on and saw still more of the island. Tattering sheets of Spanish Moss hung from trees. In some branches there were Ghost Orchids, with flowers that bloom through the night. These islands (they call them hammocks) are small, but some creatures live and die on them and know no other place.

Around the island, there were spreading fields of grass and under them, a thick mushy muck. When the skies were dry, like now, more of the muck appeared each day. The fields grew wider. The islands were no longer islands.

The sun moved low in the sky. The day was nearly gone. The little rat had no idea where he was. Or where home was.

He climbed up onto a fallen rotting tree, and hoped he might see home from there. The old log was patched with moss, dark green, white green. Dead dusty weeds, curled and knotted, clung to the bark. A cool wind blew back the leaves overhead and let sunlight pour over him.

There was a call, a yell, "Ossie!" He knew that voice, he turned—"Ossie, look out! Hawk!" And a huge dark bird dropped from the clouds.

The little rat leaped from the log and, this time, the hawk did not have him. The bird flew off toward open marsh, to look for other meals. Ossie squeezed under the rotting log. His heart hammered, his breath was quick, and he could smell the hawk still. He knew his father wouldn't be happy. If Ossie was lucky, he'd get a good long chewing-out. If he was lucky.

But his father just said, "Now you know what a hawk is."

The little rat huddled, trembled.

THE TALE OF THE SWAMP RAT

His father looked at the brittle brown weeds, nosed them, sniffed them. "Look at these things. You'd think they were dead, wouldn't you?" he said. "But they're alive. When the rain stops, like it has, they pretend to die. When the rain comes again, they open. They'll be green and beautiful. Resurrection Fern, that's what we call em."

Ossie crawled out from under the ferns and the log. And his father only said, "I used to know a rat like you." He started walking and Ossie followed. "He was about your age, when he was young. Same size, maybe bigger, maybe not. He was called Hitch and he could find trouble, anytime, anywhere. He could find trouble where there wasn't any. *There goes Miz Rat*, folk would say, *proud mother of eight fine children—and Hitch. Poor Hitch,* they'd say, *more curiosity than sense,* they'd say. *Much, much more. In fact,* they'd say, quiet, so not to make the mother feel worse than she did, *Hitch has no sense at all.* It was true. Hitch had no sense to speak of."

The Rat-Father took a sheltered cautious path, around, among tree roots, away from open ground. "I'd forgot about him till just now, till you reminded me." Ossie stayed close. "I'll tell you what folk told him. Keep a watch on where you are and where you're goin, cause soon you'll have to find your own way."

The little rat wondered at this. Find his way where? What place was he going to? Would he go there alone? Why would he have to find his *own* way?

CHAPTER 3

LEGEND

Mightiest Eagle to humble Flea,
From Pusslegut to Manatee,
Here is the one thing each thing knows:
"As goes the Gator . . . so the Swamp goes."
These are the words of the Master of Breath,
Who walks the Path from birth to Death.
—from "The Song of the Swamp"

The Rat-Father brought his son back and the other children hadn't even noticed Ossie was gone. The Rat-Mother saw that her littlest one was tired and thirsty. She took the Rat-Pups to drink. They crossed a grassy field and reached water and the young ones went running, all at once.

Until their mother yelled at them to *Stop!*

And they stopped.

What're you doin? she asked them.

Goin to drink, they answered. *We're thirsty.*

Then it'll be your last one, she said. *Look there.*

They looked. They saw nothing.

Look closer, she said. *You see a log, floatin.*

They saw a log, floating.

Now look closer still, she said. *You see that the log has eyes?*

They saw.

Do logs have eyes? she asked.

Yes, said one, *they do.*

No, she said, *they don't.*

I meant, yes they don't, he said.

But gators do, she said. *He's smart, the alligator, and he waits for those who aren't. This is not a good time to drink.*

Just then, a fish swam too close and the alligator snapped, like that, and it was the end of the fish. The gator was a monster, three feet long at least. He turned and swam off and the Rat-Mother said,

Allright, children. Now you can drink.

And the little ones drank, quickly, and didn't much enjoy it.

The Rat-Father told them that gators were worth being afraid of. Gators could grow bigger than any of the swamp folk, near big as trees, and their teeth were sharp and the bite was fast, too fast to get away from. The one they'd just seen was a baby.

Their father told about Uncle Will, the oldest and biggest of all alligators. Folk said no bigger gator ever lived. They said he was twenty-five feet long, nose to tail. They said he was six hundred years old, maybe more. There were those who believed he had walked the swamp since the day the swamp began.

They said Uncle Will saw everything. Nothing happened without his knowing. He was in every place at every moment. *Be good, y'hear me?* parents told children. *Uncle Will is out there, always watchin*. In the night, the young scared each other with tales about him.

The story of Uncle Will's life, beginning to end, is told in the song, The Song of the Swamp. Any mole can tell you the Song. Each of us learns it when we are very young. We learn every word and there are many and the words are always changing.

What a thing it would be to see that beast, Ossie thought, to see it even once. He wanted to know more. Where did it live? Had his father seen it? His mother? Had they talked to it? Had anyone? Where could he catch a sight of it himself?

What a thing that would be.

"It's late," the Rat-Father was saying now. "Let's be gettin home."

His brothers and sisters had started new games, and Ossie didn't join. He was listening again. He was listening to something distant, different.

He heard it move across a wide slough, through small tree islands, over the sawgrass. And then it moved to his island, dry and raw, setting palms clattering.

It was wind. It was a sorrowful wind, a mournful, wretched wind, and Ossie shivered against it.

THE END OF THE BEGINNING

As the last light of the day began to fade, the Rat-Mother and Rat-Father took the young rats back to the lodge. Their nest was built many seasons ago and it formed a muddy round mound of twigs, bark, roots, broken bits of creeper vine. The whole place smelled of wet, of earth, of rat. To Ossie it smelled of home.

But as night came, he heard again that same lonely wind. And again he was scared, even here. He huddled among shadows, waiting for it to pass. But it never did. It only grew louder and lonelier. Mother and Father were busy with the other children. None of them heard it.

That's when a terrible thing happened.

At first no one knew what it was, this thing that was happening. The twig room was rumbling; it might have been a storm. But the sky was clear. The walls shook and before anyone could do anything, it was there.

It was the one they called Mr. Took, a rattlesnake, huge and horrible. Stretched out he would have been ten feet, longer than many of the gators. His gut was as big around as a gumbo-limbo tree. His face was battered and bent. His slit eyes were little and mean. He was the swamp's one true monster.

And now he was here. Ossie heard his mother and father yell to the children to run, but run where? Mr. Took was in the room with them. The snake began thrashing, tearing at the walls of the lodge. The roof crumbled, holes opened, and the sky was there, but there was no moon and the room was black and full of screams.

Ossie ran to get away, but there was nowhere to go. The snake was everywhere. There were fewer screams, and fewer still.

Suddenly there was pain in his shoulder and Ossie thought it was the snake. But a stick had dropped from the ceiling, cutting deep into his back. He felt cold burning as he began to bleed. He yelled out for his mother and his father—and the snake whipped around on him. Ossie saw an ugly glow in those ugly eyes. He knew the demon was going to strike and that would be the end of it.

But then the whole ceiling fell! Twigs and mud crashed to bury Mr. Took. It wouldn't stop him long, but it was enough time for Ossie to scratch and claw his way up and over the snake and out through what had been the roof.

He was in the night and he remembered his mother's call to run and he ran. He didn't look back. His own breath choked him. The cut pounded his shoulder.

At last he stopped. Behind him he saw that yellowing eye.

The snake was coming still. No matter how fast or far Ossie ran, Mr. Took was there.

The little rat could not go much longer, he knew that. He reached the deep channel and there wasn't anywhere left to run.

He jumped into the black swamp and the pain hit his shoulder once more. He paddled and splashed and kicked to open water, half swimming, half drowning. He looked and saw the last of Mr. Took slide into the water. Ossie stopped. He wanted to sink so the snake wouldn't have him.

But as he waited, he felt a pull of current under him. A monstrous shadow formed on the water. Ossie had no idea what was happening and no time to wonder. The whole swamp washed over him and he saw nothing more.

CHAPTER 5

THE GHOST ORCHID DANCE

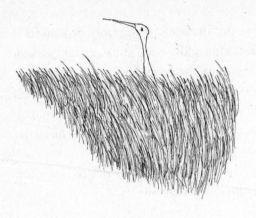

The old Alligator does not forget, not now and he never will,
He remembers the tribe Calusa, he remembers Ivory Bill,
He remembers the Ancient Elephant,
he remembers the taste of the Sea,
He remembers all that has ever been and all that is yet to Be.
—from "The Song of the Swamp"

O ssie woke, alive and in a new place. His fur was dry. He'd been here awhile. His shoulder was a swollen burning knot. He shook from fever, with shivering twitches.

It was dark. Above him Ghost Orchids flew, one tree to the next, light as sparrows. He heard them laugh. He was sure. It was a game they were playing, a game of chase. No, it was more like a dance. As they danced, they whispered among themselves. *Who's that and where'd he come from and why's he here and when's he goin?* Ossie heard them say. *Looks like Will's done it again. Will's done what again? He's gone and brought that little one back. Back from where? Back from the world of the dead! He's plucked that child from the mangroves' grasp!*

Ossie wasn't imagining this. He couldn't be.

But he looked again and no one was there. The orchids were no more than flowers, and a light breeze moved among them. How had he gotten to this place? How had he gotten out of the water? He had no idea. He closed his eyes and fell back into sleep.

When he woke again, it was day and a log watched him from the water, through two dark eyes like logs don't have. Quiet, still, unblinking eyes. Then there was a long flat snout and slowly the rest. It lifted from the swamp, more of it and still more. It was tremendous.

Ossie had never seen Uncle Will, but it had to be him. This was a thing of legends. As the great alligator moved, the world paused and looked in awe. Insects stopped buzzing and watched. Birds held to their places in the sky and saw it happen. Even clouds did not move. Or that is how it seemed.

The gator went to a spot not far from Ossie. Big as he was, and he was big as a fallen tree, he moved as simply as a lizard. He stopped now and settled to the ground, with a loud outrush of breath. Ossie felt the earth shake under him.

The little rat knew that gators eat little rats, but he was too sick to do anything. He smiled. There wasn't much from the gator, only a grunt, a grumble, and, "How you doin, boy?"

Ossie looked at him and said nothing.

"I'm not goin to eat you, if that's the issue. I've had things stuck between my teeth, bigger than you."

The little swamp rat took a step back, scared, and the gator saw and he said, "Didn't mean to spook you, boy."

Ossie said nothing.

"Guess you're not much for talkin."

Ossie looked.

The gator said, "I got no problem with that." Then he asked, "You can move, can't you?"

Once more, there was no reply.

"Well, come on then. Follow me."

The gator started off down a path and Ossie did not follow. A little farther on, the gator stopped. He settled to the ground and said, "I'm in no hurry. I can wait, patient as a buzzard." And he waited, patient as a buzzard.

Ossie got up, slowly, and took a step down the path. The alligator started moving again, ferns falling flat under him. Ossie followed the wide muddy path, as wide as his house had been. He saw this was a new island, bigger than the one he'd known. The gator's voice rumbled, a deep voice, a thousand-year-old voice. "Folk call me Uncle Will. You can, too."

Ossie didn't answer.

"Or not, as you like."

The cypress grew tall and thick here. Tangling vines hung everywhere, shining with yellow flowers. The ground was cool and mist flowers bloomed all around. Above, it closed in until the sun was blocked. Only small speckling light found its way to the swamp floor, a red-brown mulch of tree and plant pulp. After a while, they came to what seemed the center of it. Here the treetops held back. The sky was open and pure and the air was cool. A perfect round pond lay under the cypress. Its water was coppery and deep, not like the moody mud Ossie had known.

The gator looked to the pool. "Go clean the cut, boy." But Ossie didn't; he'd been warned; check the water first. Then there was a noise like wind, and the alligator's tail whipped around into him.

Ossie went flying and flipping and landed, splashing. He turned, he twisted before he found the surface and found air. He could see the old alligator smiling.

The little rat was exhausted when he climbed from the water, and Uncle Will told him, "Now rub some mud on. It's wet and cool and it'll pull the burn from your wound."

Will raked one huge wide claw across the pond shore, long and slow, and the ground was wet and cool and muddy. Ossie did as the gator said. He got the shoulder covered with mud and Will was right. The burning left the cut.

But the effort left the swamp rat worn-out. "Looks like you could use a rest," was the last Ossie heard for a while.

He fell into ugly sleep with ugly dreams. Now and then, he would wake to see an egret fly over or hear a breeze in the mossy trees. He'd tremble from fever and, in another moment, sleep was on him again. He didn't know how long it went on—hours, was it, days or weeks? He could only guess at the life going on around him, without him.

But there slowly came a time when sleep was easy. Then came a time when he stayed awake longer. He would crawl to the pond to drink and crawl back into warm sleep. Each day, he was a little more a part of the world, a little less apart from it.

In those still and quiet times, Ossie would lie and study the forest. The cypress trees were powerful things that brushed the sky. The air wore a flowered smell. Ossie never saw another creature come into this place.

It seemed to be an everlasting secret.

Each day or so, the old alligator would return. "How you feelin, boy?" he'd ask.

Each day, Ossie made no move to answer. And that was fine.

Another day, the little rat came out of a bad dream and saw the giant. The gator looked at him through eyes that had watched a million days go by and he said, "How're you feelin, Ossie?"

Ossie, the gator called him. But how? How did he find out? Who told him? Maybe Uncle Will *did* know everything. Maybe he *was* everywhere at once. Maybe the songs were true.

The gator moved off now, heading back to the swamp water. But he stopped and said, "A little mole told me."

Ossie closed his eyes and when he opened them, it was night. And Ghost Orchids danced in the sky.

CHAPTER 6

OUR SUN, SETTING

Not a thing endures but what's in an Alligator Dream.
—a swamp saying

A swamp has secrets and keeps them well. But I can tell you one. It is this. Every sunset has its sound. Folk stop to watch sunsets, that's true, but they almost never listen. And that's too bad. In the swamp, a setting sun is a glorious noise.

They're different, each one. They begin as the sun sinks to deep orange, yellow, red. That's when most of the big birds head for the roosts and there's a sound worth hearing. The night-birds take their place and it's a whole other sound.

Then it's First Dark, when the sun is gone and the moon is there, but it isn't day and it isn't night. Some of the bugs shut down, others get started. At True Dark, frogs begin their Evening Song.

These are some things you'll hear. If you listen hard, you'll hear the water hurry faster in the cool dark. You might hear night orchids open. You might hear a lot of things. It's like that, our sun, setting.

Ossie was there, watching this sunset and listening and he found his thoughts going back to that night and the snake. He only half-understood what had happened, no more than half. He knew it was bad and something had been lost to him. Yes, he knew that much.

And then, all at once, it came to him. Without warning, the whole thing came to him: His family was gone—his father, his mother, all his sisters and brothers. He was alone, just him, only him, by himself, and always.

CHAPTER 7

IN A LAND OF WOOD SAGE

Another day, Uncle Will was back. Again he asked how the little rat was. Ossie nodded, a small nod. Better, he meant to say.

A long minute went by. Then Will said, "When you feel like goin, you'll know the way."

It was more question than not and Ossie shook his head, no. He would not know the way.

Will let out a breath, a sigh, quiet and slow. The truth was this. The alligator was not young. He was not as old as the songs would have him. But he was not young. He was settled in his life and happy with it. The time for taking care of little ones was past, is what he thought.

There were days, a few, when Will didn't go back to the is-land. Instead he went swimming, adding up reasons to leave the boy there and get on with things.

But even as he thought of turning away, Will was heading back. The child would not go through this on his own.

"You know, I made this place," Will told the rat, "I made it myself."

And it was true. I can tell you it is.

This pond they call a Gator Hole. In dry times, alligators wallow in the muddy dirt until there's a pit. When the pit is deep enough, water from under the ground will seep in. In time, the hole will fill. In time, it will be a pond.

Plants will grow in the muddy banks and circle the pond. Bugs will crawl through the plants and mice will eat the bugs. Snakes will eat the mice, and on it will go. The trees will grow full and birds will fly among them. That is how it has always been. That is how it will always be.

"If the whole swamp goes dry," Will said to Ossie, "you just got to remember this place. You just got to come back to it. It'll always be here for you."

The little rat nodded. He would remember.

Toward afternoon, Will nodded off.

Ossie saw the alligator sleeping. At first he kept his distance. Then he got curious. He built up his courage and went closer. And closer still. Uncle Will was deep in some sleep-world and the little rat could only just hear his breath. He moved along the length of the gator, snout to tail, and around the other side. It was a long walk. The gator's eyes were shut and Ossie wanted to see him, close. He wanted to understand how this giant worked. He put his front paws on Will's nose.

The gator still slept. Ossie crawled onto him. Still he did not wake. Ossie crawled farther. That's what he was doing when the gator roared.

And a roar is what it was. It was a huge sound, an impossible sound, a rumbling bellow worse than thunder. The whole swamp shook from it. The little rat was so scared, he ran straight into a tree. He fell back, not moving.

The gator was awake now. "Did I scare you, boy?"

Ossie nodded, slow, dizzy. Yeah, a little. Enough to make him think the world had ended. No more than that.

"I was daydreamin," Will said and said nothing else.

He turned and left and Ossie stayed as he was. Ossie could tell there was something more, some secret the old gator was keeping.

And he was right. It was this.

In all the world there's nothing so particular as an alligator's dream. They are wonderful, terrible things. No living creature dreams the way an alligator does, and that's how it should be. Those sorts of dreams are best left to gators.

When Uncle Will dreamed, he slept deeper than other folk. His dreams took him places most never go. (That's where he was when Ossie woke him.) A gator's memory stretches past himself, back to an ancient past. A father of Will's father saw things and did things and remembered them. He passed the memories down. His children remembered them and his children's children, and their children beyond. Finally, the memory came to Will and he remembered, too.

These memories are not passed down as stories, not traded with words, but through dreams, one dreamer to the next. As a fish comes into the world knowing to swim, an alligator is born remembering. It is as simple as that. There are things in those big lizard brains that have been there since time began.

The days went as they will and one day Ossie saw wood ibis fly over and soon young ones were among them. He wondered how long he'd been here. The heavy swamp forest hid sound from him and, in this place, time moved as fast or as slow as you wanted.

At last he could walk and he went foraging food. A giant mahogany tree lay fallen across the path, felled long ago by a hurricane rage. Ossie climbed onto it, over it, out on a thick limb. It was near rotted through and he felt it give under his own slight weight.

He jumped down and came to a spot where the forest opened to a spreading field of ash-purple flowers. These were the clustered bloom of wood sage, swaying, moving, rippling like water in a slow wind. He could not take his eyes from it. The field went on and on, like nothing he had ever seen, like nothing that had ever been.

If a place like this was possible, Ossie could only imagine what else was in that world out there. . . .

CHAPTER 8

THE PREACHER BIRD

Change comes on wind, the swamp folk say,
And all things change—that is the Way,
But one thing does not change, I'll share it with you,
The single truth, forever true.
True in dark, true in light, hour of peace and hour of strife:
"The swamp is a River of water and the river of
*   Water is Life."*
These are the words of the Master of Breath,
Who walks the Path from birth to Death.
                                    —from "The Song of the Swamp"

Toward the middle of the next morning, on a day in
early Spring, the old alligator came by and didn't find
Ossie at all. Then he heard and saw him at the top of a

tall cypress, a tree much taller than the rest. If Ossie could climb a tree like that, Will knew he was better. Much better.

"What you lookin for, boy?" the gator called up.

The swamp rat didn't answer. Whatever it was, he couldn't find it.

Below him the sawgrass prairie was broad and open and stretched as far as he could see. Wide patches of the grass were yellow and brown and fallen flat from dryness. In the tree around him, up here where the sun beat hard, the leaves were withered and dead. A hot breeze rolled through and the leaves clattered and some of them fell. Ossie couldn't understand that it should not have been this way—not in the middle of the morning on a day in early Spring.

The swamp was dry, very dry.

Ossie made his way down and the cut in his shoulder left him stiff. He was near the bottom when he slipped and dropped from the tree, but fell to soft mulch.

"Your folk ever warn you about rat snakes?"

Ossie shook his head, no.

"They would've told you, watch out. A rat snake'll eat most anythin, but he's got a special cravin for rat. Little rats. Little rats who don't see where they're goin half the time."

Ossie listened, and closely.

"You're curious, boy, and that's good. So long's you don't have more curiosity than sense," the alligator said. "I'm not namin any names, Ossie. But you got to keep a watch on where you are and where you're goin, or you're goin to end up in a snake belly."

Ossie knew these words, he'd heard them before. He nodded now and his shoulder was sore from climbing. He drew it

THE TALE OF THE SWAMP RAT

up. Uncle Will checked it and said, "Looks like you'll have a mark there, for a while anyway."

The alligator told Ossie to climb onto his shoulder. But the little rat did not. He remembered another gator and a fish and— "Come on," Will said. "It's allright." And Ossie understood, somehow, that it was. He crawled onto Will's shoulder, slowly.

The old alligator moved to the wide slough and eased into the swamp water with less than half a ripple. Ossie held tight. But Will wasn't going under. They glided to deep water.

It's here that I get stopped. *Are you sure, Little Mole?* I get asked. *Are you sure this rat rode with the alligator?*

I'm sure, I say. But they don't believe me. They think I've made the thing up. I know they think that.

So I ask them, Why would a gator make friends with a rat?

Yes, why? they always say.

And I ask them, Why would an old gator care what happened to this little fellow?

Why? they ask me. *Why would he?*

And I say, Allright. Let me get to that part.

The rat didn't know where the gator was going. But in time, he understood. They weren't going anywhere and getting there was what mattered. Will was headed no special where. He was just taking things in. So Ossie took them in, too.

There wasn't much water in the swamp, but the deeper channels were still running and the two of them moved along, no more hurried than a Spring wind. This was a big place, and the alligator was going to show the child all of it.

There was something Uncle Will wanted to show Ossie. It was the thing called change—the thing that was coming to their world. Change is very hard to see, yet still they went looking.

They moved past deer in the thick-grown grass. Otters dove and darted. There were raccoon, water snakes, a bear. They saw more trees weighed with nesting ibis, they watched long-legged egrets fish the shallow swamp streams. They saw heron, sand turtles, woodpeckers. The unsoiled white of an egret's wing flashed over the scrub trees like lightning.

This was the world and it made Ossie dizzy. Not one thing was like another. They came to the rookery, the nesting trees, every limb heavy with ibis. Even from far off, the little rat could hear the life in the trees. Ibis-Mothers called to one another, one yelling over the other.

"Who's that there? Is it? It is! Hello, Miz Branchwater! How was your trip, sweetheart?"

"Wonderful, Miz Mudwalker, sweetheart! Cept we lost our poor dear Thula. Must've been halfway home when a fierce storm whipped out of nowhere. Our poor dear Thula got carried off by the horrid wind! My only beloved sister, gone like that. Dreadful loss. Didn't know how I'd carry on. Didn't think I'd have strength to see me through the grievin. Still, life continues, does it not? Your trip was better, I hope."

"Miz Branchwater, sweetheart. Thula is here, sittin not three trees from me. You just got separated from her."

"Oh. Well. Tell her Sis says hey."

Will moved below the trees. Ossie looked on the birds, in wonder. He envied them their busy, crowded lives. There were so many things to concern them, important things. Things that needed to be talked about. The gator and the swamp rat passed by, unnoticed.

They swam a channel that edged a low sawgrass field and the field was swept by silent winds. In the center of it, an egret stood, hot white on the dreary field. The bird stretched, twisting, for the sound or smell of food. Ossie was bewildered by it, by the neck as thin as a grass blade, hardly enough to hold up that head.

They went on and the big gator had a way of swimming so slow and quiet, he was barely there. If you looked, you wouldn't see him. If you listened, you'd never hear him. Maybe that was why folk thought he was everywhere at once. Maybe that was why they made up songs.

The sun moved higher and still they drifted.

Somewhere beyond the grassy field, the channel took them near a small hammock with a few tired old trees on it and nothing else. But then there was a voice—from somewhere. "My, my, my, my, my, my, my." Ossie looked and couldn't see who was doing the talking.

"Ever'day is hot and the next one hotter still," the voice was saying now. "Hot and dry, dry and hot!" Finally Ossie saw, on the limb of a weathered tree was a weathered heron. He was a big bird, blue faded to gray, and his beak had the look of old wood, his feathers always in a state of agitation.

"Mornin, Will," the bird said, eyeballing the little rat, but not saying anything.

"Mornin, Preacher."

"Fine mornin it is," Preacher said, staring at the rat and waiting. It was a long wait. Then the bird went on. "Little hot, little dry. Otherwise, we been havin an exceptional day."

"Won't argue that," said Will.

"Like as not, the rest should be exceptional, too."

"Like as not," the gator said. And said nothing more.

"Yesterday was also exceptional!" the bird added suddenly. "And the two days before!"

Will nodded a slow gatorly nod.

The bird was getting ruffled. "We've been havin a regular run of exceptional days!" he said, shouted.

Again Will said nothing, pleasantly.

"Will," the big bird said, exasperated now, "I reckon you know there's a rat on your back."

"I know. His name's Ossie."

"Yes," the bird said, relaxing finally. "Ossie. His name's Ossie. How you doin, Ossie?"

And Ossie looked to Will.

The bird said, "Not a big talker, is he?"

"He gets by, Preacher."

"He gets by," Preacher said, repeated. "We all get by, Will."

The gator told Ossie, "That's Preacher."

Let's say this. Let's say Preacher was *different*. When you first met him, you thought he was lost in some other time, his mind somewhere other than here. Then you saw, he was *different*. He was just like that. He lived on a schedule entirely his own, at a pace only he understood. But he did it well. He moved through his life with easy good manners, some sort of leftover dignity.

The bird spoke up, bright and loud, like he was breaking a

42   THE TALE OF THE SWAMP RAT

long silence, which he wasn't. "S'pose you guess what just happened to me!"

But he waited for no answer.

"I'm here, mindin my own bidness and what-all and not thinkin about what I had for dinner this noon—but what I didn't! Which was a garfish. I was thaaaaaat close to gettin me a big beautiful gar to eat. And you know what happened?"

"No, Preacher, I don't."

"Big ol bullfrog let out a croak like you never heard."

Will knew you had to let Preacher talk. Sooner or later his story would find its way back where it meant to be.

"It was Big Joe who let out that croak. Had to be Big Joe. I'm sure it was Big Joe. Who else but Big Joe? Yeah, it was Big Joe." And to Ossie he said, "The two most ornery things in the world is Wildfire and Big Joe. Only one of em is a reasonin sort, *and it ain't Big Joe.*" Preacher shook his head at the memory of it. "That frog let out a swamp-shakin croak and scared off ever'thin between here and next Spring. Anyway, I had pussleguts for dinner this noon."

The pusslegut is the smallest fish in the swamp.

"Pussleguts! That's what I'm mindin my own bidness about. And what do you reckon comes right under me?"

"What was that?" Will asked. You couldn't hurry Preacher, or he'd lose all track of his story.

"A snake. A big old copperheaded snake."

Ossie was having trouble following. The whole thing was making him sleepy.

"Anyway," Preacher went on, "this one was uglier'n usual, which is sayin somethin. All those fellas give me the creeps. But this day was goin along so nice, I didn't care. I smiled and I said, 'How you doin, friend?' You know what he did, Will?"

"You tell me, Preacher."

"Turned around and give me a big ugly hissin and called me nasty names and what-all." Preacher shook his head over it. "I won't repeat it in front of the boy. Ossie, his name is. All I say is 'How you doin, friend?' and that snake gets riled up! Why do you reckon, Will?"

The alligator said, "These're difficult times, Preacher. Most all folks are gettin edgy."

The bird just sort of hmphed and furry feathers drifted off. "I say the underlyin cause is a basic snake-ness."

But Will knew it was more. The dryness was changing everyone in the swamp.

"The problem with snakes," Preacher was going on, "is they don't stop and enjoy things like us. Look how a snake takes it easy—wrapped up in a coil! Look how a snake is when he's goin to kill you—wrapped up in a coil! Now which is which? They're mad when they're happy and happy when they're mad!"

"Snakes are funny."

"And consequently I don't care for em."

This is where Preacher and Will were different. Will had room for the snakes. But the bird had it out of his system. He was calm and his feathers fluffed on their own.

"Know what snakes can't do, Will?"

"What, Preacher?"

"Well, lot of things, flyin included. But the primary thing they cannot do . . ." The bird drifted to silence here, angling his face to the sun and saying, "The primary thing they cannot do is *this*," and the alligator knew what he meant. Preacher sat there, enjoying the world he'd been born into. That's what it was. Life wasn't easy, he seemed to say, but we'd been given these countless moments of grace, there for the taking. There to enjoy. "That's what snakes cannot do," the old bird said.

The gator nodded. "Amen, Preacher."

First Dark was on them, but they didn't go back to Will's island. The gator took Ossie to a new place, closer in, where there was an old alligator nest. It was like a rat lodge, many times bigger.

"Don't know precisely," Uncle Will said, "how a rat makes a rat-nest. But I reckon, between the two of us, we'll approximate somethin passable."

Will began digging. Ossie watched and saw how the gator worked. The little rat began digging, too. Before much longer, together they had burrowed a new home for Ossie. It was nothing special, not so nicely made as a real home. But it had a roof and walls and it worked.

When they were done, Will started for the channel. He passed a pond apple tree, half-dead. "These are troublin times," he told Ossie. "We've had dry seasons before, but this one's too dry."

Ossie was confused. There seemed to be plenty of water, whole wide streams full of it. Will showed him the pond apple tree, told how its trunk had once been underwater. The soil around it was dry and now, each day, the dryness stretched deeper into the earth.

Still Ossie didn't understand. The channel was deep, there was water everywhere, wasn't there?

Will had been around longer and he knew the moods of the swamp. He could tell things would get worse before they got better.

. . .

The little rat didn't know this world sees two seasons, one wet, one dry. The dry times are never easy. Food is hard to find. Some folk up and leave altogether. Some folk stay and try to wait it out. Some don't last to the Spring rains. They dry up like the land, turn to dust, and blow away. For those that hold on, life in the swamp moves at a sleeper's pace.

When the wet time comes, the swamp stumbles back awake. The wandering ones return. Others come out of hiding. The beat of the forest heart quickens once more.

But when a dry time stretches a year and beyond, it brings long seasons of suffering. We wait for the rain and we wait, wait, wait.

This was the start of one of those times and Will knew it.

The gator said, "Some folk think the swamp's a lake, some think it just sits. But that's not how it is. The swamp doesn't sit. It needs new water, all the time, to keep it alive. Look close, boy."

Ossie looked close. Uncle Will shook the water bugs off. "The swamp is a river of water, wide and pure. It's always movin." Ossie saw that it was. The water plants swayed to the pull of an endless current. "Even as we move through, it's movin around us, over us, under us. It never stops."

They headed on through the warm Spring afternoon and the land grew drier still.

CHAPTER 9

THE PROPHET BUBBA

The fact is, Bubba was a lonely bird. He had no family, no real friends. He had the attention of crowds, but nobody to talk with. He spent a lot of time alone, on a small hammock a few miles east of here. I guess it was there that things came to him. That's where he had his visions and his whatnots.

Sitting for days and days, alone in a tree, Bubba's mind would fill with thoughts, sooner or later. And with no one to tell them to, these thoughts turned into whole conversations he held with himself. After a while, the conversations ran in big circles, the thoughts catching up with themselves and ending where they'd started. It's a good way to go a little crazy, like that.

And another thing.

Being there, for days and days, alone in a tree, he had nobody to please but himself. And he was very pleased with himself. He was downright happy with himself. Other folk irked him.

One afternoon, the Prophet Bubba was settling into a long nap. And right as he was having it, out of nowhere, a dozen egrets flew in and flopped down on branches over him. They hadn't even seen him, just flopped in and started gabbing like egrets will. Bubba did not enjoy having his nap ruined. He did not enjoy it one bit. He growled something about the *feather-brained fools* and flew off to find a lonelier place.

"How's I s'posed to foretell the future," the Prophet asked himself, "when the present is interrupted?"

"I flat-out can't," he answered himself.

"That's all there is to it," he agreed with himself.

He found another tree and found his way back into the nap. This was yesterday.

Today, the Prophet Bubba was not alone. He had flown across the swamp to a midsized hammock and as soon as he landed, the word spread. Folk came from every inch of that island to hear what he had to say. They dropped what they were doing, then and there. *"Hurry up, Lamar, ol Bubba has arrived." "Get a move on now, the Prophet ain't goin to be here all day!" "Fetch Cousin Torbett, tell him Prophet Bubba is among us."*

With the swamp as dry as it was, they listened to Bubba more and more. Whatever he had to say, they wanted to hear it. Even doubters came now. They doubted he was right, but they weren't sure he was wrong.

The Prophet Bubba found a nice stump and sat as they gathered. He didn't talk to any of them, not yet, not a word. They brought him gifts, fish mostly, and he'd nod when a big gar dropped on the pile. *Mmmm-hmmm,* he'd say, very softly to himself.

Not much longer, everybody was there. They waited, in silence. Even the little ones knew to keep quiet.

The old Ironhead Stork was nodding now. He seemed about to speak.

"Bubba," one of them dared to say, "when is this drought goin to end?"

It was a crotchety old skunk. The Prophet Bubba raised an eyebrow at him. Then he answered.

"When it rains."

They murmured among themselves. *"He has a point." "That's true." "The Prophet's right again."*

Bubba the Prophet went on. "And just when, you ask, will the rain come? Listen to me and I'll tell you!" You could've heard a tick toot in the silence then. "The rain'll come when the clouds come. And the clouds'll come when folk quit disturbin the Forces of Nature."

They were murmuring again. Which folk? Who was doing what? They didn't know anybody had been disturbing the Forces of Nature. This was the first they'd heard of it.

Bubba harrumphed and got their attention back where he wanted it, on him. "Let me clarify. We've got a problem with folk, specially bird-folk, specially egrets. They're bein specially floppity."

Yes, of course, they whispered. The bird-folk, it was their doing. They were floppity, weren't they?

Then they quietly wondered what *floppity* meant.

The Prophet Bubba enlightened them. "There's been a highly incessant flappin-of-wings in the swamp. This wing-flappin creates air currents, same as a swimmin fish creates water currents. When enough bird-folk are flappin, it makes for a fierce wind. And that wind keeps clouds from settlin over us."

The crowd considered it. "Makes sense," one said. "The fella's a genius," somebody said. "Certifiable, he is." "What would we do without our Bubba?"

"How're we s'posed to fix this situation?" somebody called out.

"Simple," said Bubba, simply. "Bird-folk goin to have to start walkin."

A sound of a sort of surprise went over the island. "That's not possible, Bubba!" "That won't work!" "Bird-folk got to fly!" But Bubba the Prophet held his ground.

"You want this drought to last forever!?"

They were quiet. They shook their heads, no.

"You want to perish of dryness?"

Bubba saw it in their eyes. He saw the fear. This was fine. This was just what the Prophet wanted to see!

"If you don't want to die, you do as I say!"

"Allright, Bubba," they muttered, they mumbled, "we will, Bubba, just tell us what to do."

"You, bird-folk!" the Prophet Bubba shouted. "You're gonna have to stop flyin. This goes for all y'all—big birds, little birds, every bird! And you bug-folk, too. Your wings blow the clouds away, same as birds. I want to see ever'body walkin, down to the last run-of-the-mill chizzlewink." (The chizzlewinks, who did not consider themselves run-of-the-mill, were small white flies who flew in great swarms.) "This goes for bees and mosquitoes, too. You want a cure for this drought, you do what I say."

There was a long quiet moment then, a moment full of horror.

"There," said the Prophet. "I've given you the truth. Let's see what you do with it." And with that he flew off.

They tried, most of them, to live by his words. A lot of bird-folk tried walking. The bugs, too. I don't know how many chizzlewinks got eaten because they couldn't fly away, but a lot did. Mosquitoes, being arbitrary folk to start with, ignored Bubba's warning altogether. They flew. They flew wherever they liked. No way would they not fly.

And so the drought went on.

CHAPTER 10

AN ALLIGATOR DREAM

I t's like this, basically. The beat of a heart is the one true measure of time. The alligator swims through decades, while a dragonfly sees barely a season pass. Each measures time his own way, by his own heart's beat. The alligator's day is long and the dragonfly's day is short, and both of them live a lifetime. That's the way it has always been and will always be. It's like that, basically.

And just about now, time was starting to speed up for Ossie. In the days and weeks past, his life had gone along much like the old gator's. But now the little rat wanted to fill his days with more things, different things, rat things. Uncle Will saw it happening, so he showed the child more of the world.

One day might find them heading south to dry grassy plains. Another would take them north and west to the cypress forests, where there was still some deep water. This day they were moving into a hardwood strand, a marshy island, long and narrow and low. They rounded a curving channel and came on a chain of turtles, sunning on a fallen branch, one behind another behind another. The turtles saw the gator and went jumping, leaping, diving, in any direction.

"It is the end of us all!" "The Giant One is come to take us!" "Farewell, my beloved children!"

"Turtles," Will said, "is emotional folk."

As they moved on, Ossie found himself thinking of the girl. The one he'd seen so long ago. And only once. He couldn't even remember where he saw her. But with each new island they passed, he wondered, *is it this one? Is she here?* And in that time, he never saw her.

He might have wondered, *does she ever think of me? Does she remember that day as I do?* But he did not wonder these things.

In a while they came on an old oak, overhanging the slough. On its branches were two birds, wings wide, feathers spread out in a fan, as if the birds were frozen in midflight. They were sitting like that, not doing much but talking. They hadn't noticed the rat and the alligator.

"You heard, I guess," one said to the other.

"You guess I heard what?" the other said back.

"About the snake and what he did."

"Mr. Took?"

The first one nodded.

"The monster," the second one muttered. "What'd he do?"

"This was a few weeks back, is how I have it. Down south of here."

"What? What happened?"

"A poor rat family," the first one answered. "Twelve chirren or so, is how I have it."

"But what happened!?"

"Mr. Took got em all, is how I have it."

The second one shook her head. "The monster."

"Except one, is how I have it," the first bird added. "Isn't that strange?"

"Strange how so?"

"That Mr. Took'd let one go," the first explained.

The other nodded. "Oh, I see. Now that you say. Yes. It is strange. Very strange."

"Why do you think it was? What was it about that one? Why'd the snake let him go?"

Uncle Will had heard enough and he brought his tail up and slapped the water, *SLAAAAP!,* like that. The birds almost fell out of the tree. Startled feathers rained from them.

As the gator swam under, the first one said, "Oh, hello, Uncle," trying to sound casual and sounding not.

"Mornin, sir," the second bird coughed. "Lovely day, no? Skeeters are downright civil," she said, *skeeters* her word for mosquitoes.

"Uh-huh," said Uncle Will as he glided below. Ossie could hear their panicky breaths. The birds had wings outstretched again and every last feather trembled.

As they moved on, the swamp rat looked back.

"Those're snakebirds," Will said, to get Ossie's mind off what they'd heard. "They dive for fish, and their feathers get so wet they can't fly. They spread em out to dry. Slows em down and gives the fish a chance."

And he moved ahead, a little faster. "We got to get goin. Somethin I want to show you." But he didn't say what.

They followed a channel as it widened, and widened more. Sawgrass rose on either side, solid as any wall. A pool opened in the channel. It was deep, you could tell, because it was crowded with the plant they call Alligator Flag. The flag only grows where the swamp bottom drops off and the water runs deep. Across the pond was something huge and quiet and grown over with vine. It almost looked like a nest, but too big for any creature Ossie knew.

The gator crawled from the water and the rat hopped down. "Wait here." Will disappeared into the vines. There were grunts and bellows and a family of snakes came out, hissing and furious, copperheads, no problem for a gator, but Ossie shot up a tree. In another moment, Uncle Will was back. "Come on, boy," he said.

Ossie went with him into the strange place. It was dark as night inside and he could not see a thing.

"Used to be another sort of folk lived here," Will said. "Folk called Man."

There was a snake-smell over everything, a sour smell that made Ossie sick. He breathed slow, trying not to choke, and that's when he began to see. Things took form in the dim shadows. A huge room opened around them. Its roof was high, tall as a young tree. They were in some sort of big house.

Before Will had ever been here, he knew this place. He knew it from a dream. A father of his father had known the people who lived in this home. He told Ossie the Dream. And it was this.

A Hundred years and more ago, there were Men livin here and they were Indians. The Swamp has always known the Indian. Over time they've come, then gone, blendin one group to the next.

A Hundred years and more ago, whole new tribes came to the Swamp. They walked from the north. Among them were Slaves, run away from other Men. They came to the Swamp and were called Seminole. "Free people," it meant.

My great-great-grandfather was a boy in those days. He saw. He never forgot. And I remember it now.

The Indians made houses like this, called chickees. They built their houses strong to stand the hurricane wind. They used posts of cypress to hold a roof woven of palm, open all sides, so the Swamp breeze might cool them. For year upon year, the Seminole tribes lived in the Swamp and their lives were good.

At least it was so until a time of Killin began. . . .

Other Men came to the Swamp. They wanted their Slaves back. They wanted this land for their own. They wanted the Indian to go. But the Indian would not leave. And that is when it began. The Killin time began. The Seminole Wars, they came to be called.

The fightin started one Winter day and went on and on and on. Many died, but the Seminole were never beaten.

Great chiefs rose to lead them. The tribes moved deeper into the Swamp. The other Men came after them. And the fightin did not stop.

There were seasons when the Water under the grass was red from their blood. But the Water flowed from the Swamp and the blood flowed with it.

Some Seminole left the Swamp, others moved deeper among the jungle hammocks. The others came for them. And the fightin went on. Children grew to Men and it did not stop. Year after year passed this way in War.

Then one day it stopped. It ended like that. This War, the Men saw, would go on for all Time. It would be won, they saw, by no one. The other Men left and the Indian stayed. They have stayed to this day.

Unconquered, they are called.

By the time Will and Ossie left the old chickee, the sun was low and a long flock of egrets crossed the afternoon sky. From the twisting knees of a cypress, Ossie heard the angry copper-headed curses.

The little swamp rat wondered, Why had Will told him this story? Why had the gator brought him to this place? Was it the thing he wanted Ossie to see?

The old gator seemed to understand the thoughts running around Ossie's mind. "Takes a lot of little pieces to make up this big world," is all he said.

Sometimes folks stop me at this part. They say, *Little Mole, you spend your life under the earth, under our feet.* This is true, very true. *Little Mole,* they go on, *most of the time you are alone and by yourself.* True as well. *You must get lonely there.* At times I do. *How can we know that, in your loneliness, you don't make these things up?*

I only say, you can't know.

How can we know, they ask, *that anythin you say is true?*

Again I say, you can't. But you can know this. If I have added to the story, if I have changed the way it was and made it another, I have only done this to make it more true. I hope you will take my word on that.

Sometimes Preacher came with Ossie and Will. What water there was, was shallow now and he'd wade alongside the gator. Between them, Uncle Will and Preacher knew everybody in the swamp.

"Over there's Blue Pete," Preacher would say, waving to a kingfisher. "Mornin, Blue Pete!"

And the bird would call back, "Howdy, Preacher! Howdy, Will!"

They moved by a tree full of ibis and Ossie heard whispers pass through the branches. *"Who's the rat?" "Ain't got a clue." "Never seen him before." "Not from around here." "Who's his parents?" "A Fern Child, I hear."* It was a thing swamp folk said, *Fern Child*. It meant an orphan, as they were often found hiding among sheltering ferns.

Another time they passed a black bear halfway up a fiddle-wood tree. "How you doin, Brother Bear?" said the gator.

"Doin good, Will," the bear called. Then he added, "S'pose you know there's a rat on your back?"

"Sure he knows, Bear!" said Preacher. "How's he gonna not know!?"

"Only commentin on it," the bear replied.

"The boy's named Ossie," Will said as they drifted on, and the bear said, "Nice to meet you, Ossie."

And the little rat nodded to him.

Preacher said, "Ossie's not much for talkin."

That's the way it went and the days had no end to them.

Ossie and the alligator were quietly crossing the swamp

when the little rat saw something move on a near shore. Was it her? It moved from the leafy shadow and wasn't a rat at all, but a mother possum, foraging food, babies clinging all over. Uncle Will said, "You want to go over? You want to say hello?"

Ossie shook his head no. Will let it go at that. He knew the swamp rat might live forever this way, might never go over, might never say hello.

But change, Will knew, would have to come from Ossie.

CHAPTER 11

ON THE WIDE RIVER

And change, Will saw, was coming. It came slowly, over days, over weeks. But it came.

One morning, early, Ossie was at the water's edge waiting for Will. The old gator wasn't there and he should've been. The little rat wandered the dusty shore, back and forth, and wondered why Will hadn't come yet. He climbed a tree for a better view, but the gator was nowhere to be seen. The swamp rat wanted to call out.

Around midday, Will finally showed up and Ossie raced to see him, happy he was there and mad he was late.

The gator saw and was pleased. Ossie was restless and that was good. The more restless the swamp rat grew, the more sure he became. He wasn't so scared of the world, but growing into it. In time, Uncle Will thought, things could turn out right for Ossie.

They crossed the swamp's grassy fields to a place where a deep channel flowed through an ages-old forest. And here they met Rufus.

Ossie grew shy again, even a little frightened.

Because Rufus was unusual to see. He kept mostly to the water, but he rose to the surface now, in the middle of a lily pad swath. He looked like the shadow of some other creature. He was huge, the shape of a mangled root. They say Rufus has a long-distant cousin called the Elephant. Maybe it's so. I don't know. But I do know he is unlike anyone else in our swamp.

Rufus is a manatee.

He spoke and his voice was deep and noble, watery smooth. "I known you a long time, Will."

"Long time, Rufus."

"That's why I'm goin to tell you this. You don't know, but there's a little rat on you. He's tryin to hitch a ride somewhere." Rufus had a way of knowing things were one way, when they weren't.

Will was swimming slowly on the river and the manatee moved alongside. The gator introduced Rufus to Ossie and Ossie to Rufus and Rufus said, "You're takin him to his folk."

"I, more or less, am his folk," Will explained.

"That sounds like you're raisin the boy, but that ain't what you mean."

"Yeah, Rufus, that's what I mean."

The manatee said nothing for a while, then let loose with

a laugh. It was big, one laugh tumbling out after another, each one separate and not quite like the other. The laughter did not stop, but kept growing. Birds were frightened out of their nests by it. Ducks took flight as it rolled across the swamp and echoed off clouds. It was that kind of a laugh. It did not end until Rufus began coughing.

"You done?" Will asked.

Rufus was exhausted. "I'm pretty much through," he told Will, who said, "Good."

Rufus heaved for breath. "That took somethin out of me." His face was red, but heading toward its old color. He stopped swimming, to rest.

"Son, if this old gator can't handle things, you call Rufus," said Rufus.

"Thanks for offerin," Will told him.

"Maybe this poor tired old gator can't take care of you all by hisself. Might need my help. Might even need the Sun Children helpin, too!"

And laughter, thick as morning mist, poured onto the swamp yet again. It stopped when Rufus started coughing again.

"Don't s'pose," Will said, "the boy would know who they are."

"You don't tell me! That so, boy? You don't know about the Children of the Sun?"

Ossie shook his head, no, he did not.

"Most ever'body knows about those children," Rufus said.

"Most ever'body. But not ever'body," said Will, and he told Ossie that Rufus knew all the stories and legends of the swamp. And Rufus had to admit, this was true.

"You never told him the tale?"

Will shook his head, no, he had not. Rufus was waiting and wanting to be asked to tell it and Will smiled and let Rufus wait a little longer.

"S'pose I could tell him," Rufus finally said.

"S'pose you could," Will said back.

There. That was all it took. Rufus had a nice voice and he liked to hear it. He told Ossie the tale.

The Tale of the Sun Children

Once long ago, a tribe of Man lived where the land is dry and the Pines are tall. They were a quarrelsome folk, always fightin with neighbors. One day while they were busy bickerin, a bunch of their Children wandered off and got lost in the Swamp Forest. The Mothers and Fathers started wailin and prayin to the greatest of Spirits, the Master of Breath.

"Find our Children, Master B!" they hollered, which was a cheeky thing to call the Master of Breath. "Find em and show em the way back to us!" they yelled.

Now the Master of Breath wasn't Fond of these fractious folk. So He said, "I will help your Children if you will change your ways. I'm tired of listenin to the fightin and bickerin. I want an end to it, now."

And the Men said, "We will fight and bicker no more."

So the Master of Breath set off to Find the Children, but no sooner was His back turned than He heard this. "Master B'll find em, fast as that!"

"I know! That's why I said to call Him."

"*You* said to call Him? It was my idea to call Him!"

And push led to shove and soon there was a Brawl goin on. The Master of Breath saw and said to Hisself, "That's the last straw. I won't bring the Children home just so they can grow up to fight and bicker like that."

And He left the Little Ones out there in the Swamp.

But He went to the Sun and told him to watch out for the Little Ones, see they stayed safe.

Sun said, "Yes, sir, I'll sure do that!"

The Master of Breath told Sun to let those Children wander the Swamp and search out anybody needin some Help.

Sun said, "I'll get right on it!" and he told the Children they would help the lost, the sick, and the Weak. And in this way, they would make up for the foul deeds of their folk.

They're still out there, those Little Ones.

And they are called Children of the Sun.

"And if I never saw em myself," Rufus told Ossie, "that does not mean they are not there." The little rat liked that, the thought of those children, out there, somewhere.

Late the next morning, they were near Big Cypress and the gator took Ossie to a small island that rose beside the slough. The gator said, wait here. He'd be back, he said, sooner or later. "Keep a watch on where you are," he said and he swam off and there was only forgetful rippling where he had been.

The swamp rat decided to explore by himself. It was a small island, or seemed. But the more he looked, the more he saw. He came onto a tree full of many-colored snails in endless movement, up, down, around the trunk. He climbed carefully past them and as he climbed, his shoulder loosened. He grew surefooted as he went. He jumped from branch to branch, moving quickly higher through the tree. He found himself thinking of the girl-rat, the one who saw the butterflies with him. He leaped, jumped, one branch to another and thought, *If only she could see me!*

That's how he came to land on the snake, a big fat rat snake, laid looping over a branch. He was on top of it and, somehow, the big fat lazy thing was still asleep and snoring. Ossie moved off the snake, not daring to breathe. He was scared to think, or his thoughts might wake it. He crawled quickly up and away from the snake.

A dozen feet higher, Ossie looked down. It was there still, asleep still, and that was stupid luck. By all rights, Ossie should've been in the snake's belly by then. It was pure stupid luck.

He moved on, careful now. The tree was heavy with Spanish Moss and he worked his way through an itchy clump. He heard rustling and stopped. He edged forward.

There was an egret nest. In it, three babies, strange looking, with furry fuzz. One of them, a boy, saw Ossie. "Look there," he whispered to the others, "it's a little swamp rat."

The littler of the girls started to ask, "Hey, rat, what you doin—"

"Midge! Henry!" the other, an older girl, snapped. "Don't talk to him! You know what Mother says. Mother says rats are common and crass and got no manners to speak of."

Ossie crawled closer, a bit.

"Look at that thing on his shoulder," the littler girl, Midge, whispered to the others.

"What *is* it, Sally Ann?" the boy asked the older girl.

Ossie didn't know either, not at first. He'd never seen the old cut, never thought much about it. When it quit hurting, he forgot it was there.

"It's a scar," the older girl said. "Somethin's left a mark on him."

"How'd he get it?" the boy asked.

"Rats are so base!" Sally Ann answered. "They got no breedin. They do common and crass things. I'd hate to know how he got it!"

Ossie was ashamed now.

"Why cain't we ask him?" Henry asked.

"I s'pose we could," the older girl said, "but do it quick! Rats are so base."

"Tell us, Rat. What happened to you?"

Ossie could not tell them.

"Cain't you talk?" Sally Ann said, sharply.

Ossie could feel his own face, hot from embarrassment.

"He cain't!" Midge squealed. "He cain't talk! There's somethin the wrong with him!"

And Henry said, "He's strange, that's what's the wrong with him."

"Maybe he's crazy," the littler girl said.

"He's common and crass and stupid and base," Sally Ann

THE TALE OF THE SWAMP RAT

explained, "but don't be too awful hard on him. He cain't help the way he is. Rats are born ignoramuses."

Ossie looked down. He saw only branches, but there should have been more. There should have been a snake. He hurried to a far branch and looked and didn't see the snake.

And then it was there, on the branch with them.

"Snakesnakesnake!" yelled the littler girl (because, never mind the name, a rat snake will eat a bird).

The Egret-Chicks were squealing, screeching, screaming.

Rat Snake looked on, mouth curled from disgust. "Hush, chirren!" he hissed. "That—is—enough!"

The birds quieted. The snake moved toward them, shaking his head. "Why are you so noisy? Don't you unnerstan? I'm only goin to eat one of you. Maybe rat, maybe bird. I can't eat every last one! The others will be just fine. Come mornin, y'all won't remember the one I got." He said that. That is how snakes look at the world. "So let's stop this squealin. It's ridiculous."

He was on them now. The birds were loud again and Ossie was looking for a way out.

What happened then? It could have gone a lot of ways. But what happened was a wide shadow came over them. The air was wildly whipping. It was the Egret-Mother. She was screeching, flapping, claws grabbing at the snake. She was giant, all angry noise. The Egret-Chicks drew back in the nest and Ossie was almost knocked from the tree. He couldn't get out of the way.

The Egret-Mother struck with her beak. The snake was thrashing and hissing. Ossie slipped. He fell.

But he caught himself not far below and scrambled to another branch. The fighting went on above him, twigs, feathers pouring down. And then, in another moment, the snake fell. Ossie watched it drop, breaking through branches. "Ow! Oh! Ouch! Ooo! Umph!" The thing lay on the ground a long moment, then moved slowly into the forest.

"You got a bad attitude, ma'am!" the snake yelled, distant, furious. "I wasn't goin to take em all! Just one, that's all I wanted! A snake's got to eat, you know! A snake's got needs, you know! Bad attitude, that's what you got, ma'am!" Even when he was gone, he was still cursing at her.

Ossie looked up and the Egret-Mother was watching him, the wildness still in her eyes. He thought he'd better go. And he went.

He ran.

CHAPTER 12
THE LOST CHILD

And he ran. He did not know where he was going, only someplace other than where he was. He reached a far edge of the hammock. Here the water had drawn back and there was only land between this island and the next. The little rat ran on.

Halfway between, the land wasn't as dry as it looked. Under the baked dust was a heavy oily mud. Ossie was small, light, and at first he crossed it easily. But mud began to coat his feet, and he slowed. He grew quickly muddier and it was all over him, thick stinking mud. He was miring in it.

For a time, he wasn't sure he'd make it. He could be trapped here, stuck. The sun or the birds would get him. He looked ahead. The next island was closer than the one he had left. The little rat used all his strength, and then some, and pulled himself from the mud. He chose every step carefully, finding the most solid way to drier land.

He crawled into the cool shade of the island and rested there, confused and scared. He thought he should . . . He thought he might . . .

Well, he didn't know what he would do.

He tried sorting his thoughts, but they were a mess, jumbled, heaped, in layers, like water in a stale pond. The topmost ones were panic and fear, as useless as the weedy scum on the water's top. The deeper he went, the clearer his thoughts became. Finally, under the confusion, under the dread, he found this.

He found disappointment. A deep awful disappointment with himself. He had let Will down. The gator trusted him and left him on his own and he'd made a mess of it. That's what he had done. Uncle Will warned him about rat snakes. Worse still, he almost got those birds killed, it was close.

He climbed a giant cypress knee and looked around. But he had no idea where he was.

A mess is what he'd made of things.

About then, on the other island, the old gator came to get the young rat. Ossie wasn't there and Will gave it no thought. The boy was off playing, that was all, that was fine. Then an hour passed and another on top of it. The sun was dropping. Will called for Ossie. The deep gator voice rolled over the island. But Ossie did not come.

Will set off looking.

• • •

Ossie knew Will would be looking. He had to get back. He hurried through the island, until he came onto water again. It was a full channel, but was it the same channel? He looked this way and that, but could not tell where he was. He only knew he was lost, very lost.

First Dark was on the land.

Will found Preacher and together they searched. The old heron flew to see more, more quickly. But night was covering the swamp. The shadows grew deep and became gaping holes on the landscape. In a while more, everything was buried under the darkness.

There was no hope of finding Ossie, not this night. They'd sleep and try again with the morning.

But there was no sleep for Ossie. He lay huddled among the roots of an oak, listening to the sounds of unbounded night, sounds from everywhere, without the least letup. He was caught in a nightmare, wide-awake, no getting out. Time had stopped and the night had no end.

When morning finally was there, Ossie felt he'd willed the sun to rise and was exhausted from the effort. He left the fold of the roots and went looking. He went to the channel's edge, where a giant cypress grew. Clustered around its trunk were a dozen knees. Ossie crawled onto one and looked. He didn't know what he was looking for, but he looked for something, anything familiar.

And he was still looking when a voice came at him. "Now, child, you take most rats."

He spun around fast and there was a hawk, broad-chested,

shining, sharp-clawed, sharper-beaked. It could reach Ossie, easy. There was no use running.

"Most rats," the hawk was saying, "have sense not to sit out in the plain middle of it all. But, child, I guess you're not like most rats."

The hawk saw the scar. "What happened to you?"

Ossie turned from the bird and the bird reached out a claw and pinned his tail. "Child, pay *tention* when I talk."

"Excuse me, sir," came another voice. The hawk whipped around and saw a mouth full of teeth, ready to close on him.

The bird went flying as fast as any bird flew. (And Ossie never saw it again for as long as he lived.)

"Ossie. Let's go," said Will. And they went. They drifted into the wide river that was the swamp.

Preacher walked alongside in the shallow water. "Got yourself a little lost, huh, boy?" the old bird said.

In a moment more, Uncle Will said, "You got to keep your eyes open, son, if you want to get by in this swamp."

The little rat nodded, more ashamed than before.

"Not much longer," Will went on, "and you're goin to have to find your own way."

There they were again, those words his father had told him. And still Ossie didn't understand. Was it a place he was supposed to find? And *when* would he have to find his way there?

CHAPTER 13
WHAT A NIGHT HERON KNOWS

Ossie did not have to wait for Uncle Will the next morning. The gator was there waiting for *him*. "Got to get goin, boy."

They went north, where the horizon was thick with cypress islands. They were half the way there when a jagged sound tore the air. Ossie shrunk against the gator's back. It was coming from the west, the Piney Wood. The cry washed over them, into the ancient swamp, and died in the heat-heavy air.

"You know that sound?"

Ossie did not.

"Only one fellow makes it," Will said. "And that's Panther."

The gator moved along, up a wide-flowing slough, and the trees above sagged with thick Spanish Moss. Will told Ossie, "Panther's a fine, fierce hunter, best there is. But he's

A Child of the Fern   73

a independent fellow, keeps to himself. Only met him a few times myself."

The little rat searched the forest for a sight of the creature.

"He moves through the swamp on a solitary path."

The woods were quiet. There was no wind and Ossie felt it. Without the smallest breath of breeze, the swamp was a place of infinite stillness.

"S'pose you can't blame Panther. There's not many of his kind left. He got no choice but be alone."

The swamp folk sang Songs about Panther, same as they did for Will. The Songs said Panther was half-living, half-spirit. Panther moved without sound, you could not hear him come. At night, the Songs said, he grew wings and flew among trees like Owl. When Panther went after you, there was no getting away.

The Songs said that. Will said Panther was a great hunter and Ossie should keep his distance.

The old gator followed the channel as it turned and that's when they swam into the middle of a fight. Two ibis were going at it over a fish that wasn't there, jabbing each other with long beaks.

"I had him, ya simpleminded imbecile!"

"I seen him first!" the other one said.

"Aw, you saw me see him!"

"I saw you see me see him!" the other one said.

"No, you saw me see you saw him see . . . he saw you . . . I saw me saw . . ." And then, "Just shuddup and fight."

They fought until Uncle Will swam between them. "Mornin, fellas," he said. And that ended it, fast. The birds took off, each in another direction, and Will told Ossie, "Remember I was tellin you, there's change comin to the swamp. That right there was it, more or less. That's what change looks like."

Ossie tried to see, but couldn't.

"Howdy, Will," came another voice from another tree. "Lo, Ossie." It was Preacher and he flew closer. "Smooth how you broke that up."

Uncle Will settled himself in the water, out of the hot sun. "I was tellin the boy, it's a sign of the change."

"That's so." Preacher nodded. "Surely it is."

Ossie looked confused. Ossie was confused.

"Let me explain." Preacher puffed himself up and declared, "The situation, son, is this." Ossie waited. "The situation, son, is this dryness and what-all makes folks get . . ." Preacher *worked* for the right word. "They get in-directed, if you see what I'm sayin."

Preacher was proud. *In-directed.* What a word. What a fine word. He gave the others a look to see if they liked it as much. Ossie was blank. Will was trying to find shade.

The heron shook his feathers and hmphed. "Let me explain so you'll unnerstan, son." He was riling now. The words weren't coming. "The dryness makes folks . . ." And it came! "Self-fragmentized!" Preacher grinned ear to ear, such ears as he had. "And that, my boy, is plain as I can put it!"

Ossie looked a little blanker. The alligator was settling into some cool mud. Preacher gave them a fierce look, daring them to ask for more.

Will spoke. "What Preacher is sayin, and not very well . . ." (Preacher coughed up a fish) ". . . is ever'thin changes in a dry time. Ever'body changes, too. Drier it gets, worse it gets.

There's an Unspoken Word that moves through the swamp in times like these. And the Word is *share*—take what's left and use it careful. But folk forget sometimes. They get so busy lookin out for themselves, they don't hear the Unspoken Word."

And Preacher said, "Amen."

Ossie understood.

And Preacher added, "Like I said, they get *self-fragmentized*."

They were in a wide sawgrass plain now and moving toward an island they had never been to before. "I asked around," Will said. "Asked where there might be swamp rats. Seems with the drought, there's not so many this year."

Ossie saw the landlocked island ahead of them.

"I finally found a night heron, he told me where to look."

Ossie stared hard at the island.

"The night heron knows a lot of things. They see the world when it's sleepin, when the world doesn't know it's bein seen. You got a question, ask a night heron. They'll know."

It *might* be the island, her island. It *could* be. Ossie wasn't sure. The whole thing happened so long ago.

Then Will stopped. "Sounds like there's somethin over there," he said.

Ossie looked and saw nothing.

"Deep in the woods. Listen."

Ossie listened. He heard far-off voices, the voices of young creatures.

Will headed toward the island and stopped where the water gave itself over to land. He waited for Ossie to climb off, but the boy did not. "Go on. You'll find the way."

The swamp rat shook with fear.

• • •

Here's what I think. I think Ossie was afraid that *this* was it. He thought *now* was when he'd have to find his own way. And he wasn't ready for it.

I could be wrong, but that is what I think. Still, I am no more than a mole.

"Don't be scared, Ossie," the old gator said, quietly.

And, somehow, the little rat wasn't. He went. And as he went, he did not notice that Spring was turning into Summer.

PART TWO

PAHAYOKEE,
THE GRASSY WATER

CHAPTER 14
A WORLD OF WILDPINE

"**K**eep goin," Will said again when Ossie stopped again and stood in the flat Summer sun.

There was quick rustling in the vines, things running past, deeper onto the island. Ossie headed up the dusty shore. When the swamp drained back, a hole was left here, full of thick water, cooking in the sun. It wasn't really water anymore, but something oozing, stinking, full of bloated dead fish and rotten plants, smelling worse than any skunk. In time the whole swamp would come to this.

Ossie moved around it and into heavy undergrowth. He turned to check on Uncle Will a last time.

"I'll be here or hereabout," the gator said.

Ossie climbed up roots and along a branch exploding with wildpine. The plant grew everywhere and so quickly he could nearly see it happen. The swamp rat disappeared into that world of wildpine.

Will let a leisurely current pull him back into the slough.

Ossie was on his own now. He found his way deeper onto the island and the trees grew thicker and vines tangled into bushes into flowers into more vines. It was dark and cool. Every plant grew angled, as if bent under a wind, leaning toward any sun they might find. In time, Ossie came on a small clearing. Sunlit patches dashed over the ground. The little rat stopped and listened.

He couldn't hear anything now. Whoever had been here, they were gone. He was ready to go back.

Then, fast as that, they were nearly on him—a huge messy mass of them, rolling, tumbling, falling, laughing, a dozen or more of them, animals, young ones, all kinds, everywhere. Ossie was terrified. He had to get out of there.

He dove into the bushes and they poured past. He sat there, not moving or breathing. Had they seen him? No, he didn't think so. They were gone, all of them, yes, he was sure. He better get to the shore and find Will, fast.

But just as he was about to move, one more of them was coming. Ossie crawled deeper into hiding. It was a small armadillo and he stopped just in front of the swamp rat. The fellow had a plate of thick skin over his back, but his claws were tiny as a bird's. His face was small, too, with a long thin snout. He was looking for someone, something. He checked every tree, every branch, every bush. And Ossie saw, in one terrible second, that he was coming this way. The armadillo used his snout to push the leaves aside and they were face-to-face.

"You're It," the armadillo said.

Then he called out, "Okay. The rat's It." And to Ossie he said, "Come on. You're It. I got you. Fair and square."

But Ossie stayed where he was.

The armadillo was still talking, more to himself. "We have time for another game, maybe two. Unless Stubb is It, then one. And we'll be lucky to get one. You know Stubb. Stubb's kind of slow." And again to Ossie, "Hurry up. They'll be here soon."

But Ossie stayed where he was.

Now the armadillo looked at him, close. "Hold on. Who are you?"

Ossie didn't move.

"I don't know you."

The little rat shook his head, no, you do not.

"You're not in the game."

Ossie shook his head, no, he wasn't, this much was true.

"Who are you?"

And Ossie couldn't answer.

Then the armadillo started talking to himself, a whole storm of words. Ossie watched as the fellow worked through the thing and all by himself, as if Ossie had up and left.

"We got a good dozen swamp rats on this island, maybe two dozen," the armadillo was telling himself, *"but this isn't one of em, so where'd he come from, and how'd he get here, and what's he doin in the middle of our game, that's what I got to figure out."*

Then he was talking to Ossie again. "What'd you say your name was? Oh, yeah. You didn't. So what is it?" he asked.

And once more Ossie was silent.

"You're not much for talkin, are you?"

Ossie nodded again, that much was true, very true.

"That's okay," the armadillo said. "Talkin's not such a great thing. I'm Tudd."

The others were showing up, one after another, on and on. There were a dozen of them, no, even more. There was a half-awake possum, a little owl, more armadillos, a tiny mouse, a kingfisher, a gopher turtle, a small quail with another older one, a group of tree frogs, three young swamp rats, every child from the island.

"He's new," Tudd was telling them. "He's It, but he can't be, cause he's not in the game. We don't know his name."

"Why not?"

"He's not a big talker," Tudd answered for him.

"Why not?"

"Don't know," Tudd said. "He won't tell."

They were all talking then, to him, at him, around him.

"Why can't you talk?"

"Maybe he's got a speech impediment."

"How, if he cain't speak?"

"Maybe he ain't from around here."

"DO—YOU—KNOW—OUR—LANGUAGE?"

Ossie searched the crowd. Was the girl-rat there? She seemed not to be, but he wasn't sure. There were so many of them. The owl jumped closer, a burrowing owl, all white, hardly bigger than a pinecone. "Name's Gib," he said, and bobbed as he talked, up, down, again, again, always moving, never stopping. He seemed somehow in charge of the group. Gib introduced Ossie to the others.

First there was the possum. He was asleep, but woke enough to say, "Mornin."

"Afternoon," Gib told him.

"You kiddin me?" said the possum. "When'd it get to be afternoon?"

"Right after noon," Gib said.

"Oh." Then the possum told Ossie, "My name's Bevel. Any of these fellas gives you a problem, you see Bevel. Somebody's botherin you, you see Bevel. Bevel can fix it. Bevel don't like to fight, but he fights when he has to. And nobody fights like Bevel. That's why nobody messes with Bevel."

And the white owl said, "Bevel's name ain't Bevel. It's Clavis. There ain't no Bevel, and Clavis was never in a fight, not once in his life."

"You got to unnerstan," said a toothy young rat, "Clavis don't like to tell the truth."

"That's not true," said the possum Bevel. Or, Clavis.

"And neither is that," said the armadillo Tudd.

"Clavis is a good guy," an impossibly small mouse was saying, "but you can't believe a blessed word he says."

"Come on, now!" Clavis said. "You're makin me sound like a liar."

"You are!" said three or four of them, maybe more.

"Foot!" said one of the rats, pudgy around the middle and fuzzy at the edges. "Foot! How long are we goin to stand here yammerin?" (This pudgy rat was *always* in a lousy mood, but no one seemed to pay him any attention.)

"Hullo," came a voice.

Ossie found a gopher turtle, smiling, nodding. "Name's Stubb," the turtle said.

Gib moved on and introduced more and then more, and there were names, a lot of names, too many names, and they ran together for Ossie. There were two quails, sisters, Philomena, tall and thin and quiet, and Lodemia, small and round and not.

"YOU WANT TO SEE ME FLY?" said Lodemia, sudden and loud.

"Lodemia, you cannot fly," the older sister said, soft and calm.

"I CAN!" the littler one yelled and ran and jumped and flew face-first into a tree. The *SMACK!* of it rang over the others and right into their spines. Feathers and leaves fluttered as Lodemia dropped to the ground and jumped to her feet and yelled at Philomena, "I TOLD YOU I COULD FLY!" There was already a welt the size of a sparrow egg on her forehead.

Ossie met tree frogs, kingfishers, gray squirrels. The swamp rats were brothers, three of them, about his age.

"Hullo," came a voice. Ossie found the gopher turtle behind him, again. "Name's Stubb," the turtle said, again. The rat nodded back, hello. He wasn't sure if the turtle was just friendly or had forgot they'd met.

Gib whispered, "Stubb's a little slow-gifted."

One of the Rat-Brothers saw Ossie's shoulder and asked, "What's that?"

"It's a scar," the owl, Gib, answered for him.

"Yes, uh-huh, it—it—it is a scar," said the little mouse. He was a serious, earnest creature. Maybe a week old, he already had the face he'd have all his life. His eyebrows were set in endless worry and he was tiny, too small to name. They called him *the mouse,* nothing more.

"Excuse me, but—but—but just what," *the mouse* asked, timid, "is a scar?"

"It's somethin that heals over and leaves a mark."

the mouse nodded, yes, yes of course. They moved in to see the scar and this time Ossie wasn't embarrassed.

Then Tudd said, "Aw, good Lord."

They all looked and somebody said, "It's Johnny."

"Foot!" grumbled the cranky rat.

Ossie saw another swamp rat, older and bigger than he was, with a pack of mean-looking, chewed-up rats clustered around him.

"You don't want to meet him," whispered Tudd the armadillo, "or his friends either."

"HE'S A MAMA'S BOY!" Lodemia the quail said, louder than she needed to. They told her to quiet down and she said, not much quieter, "WELL, HE *IS*."

"He is," Philomena said, "and a mean one, too."

They moved close around Ossie, hiding him from Johnny's view.

Tudd was talking again, and again to himself.

"We can't let Johnny see him," Tudd was telling himself, "a quiet little guy like this, Johnny's goin to tear him to pieces, that's how Johnny is, specially with quiet ones," he kept on, plotting the whole thing out for himself, "cause Johnny's a jerk, that's all there is to it," Tudd was muttering, "Johnny likes not bein liked, 'fact, he'd be miserable if you liked him, so we got to hide this fellow."

Johnny and the other rats moved closer. "Look," Gib quickly said, "here's the deal, we're playin chase." And they were, like that. They ran off into the forest and Johnny never saw the new swamp rat. Gib saved him from that.

They all said how the little owl was clever. They told Ossie how Gib outsmarted a King Snake once and everybody knows how smart King Snakes are, but Gib was smarter. He was alone when he ran up against a snake as long as sawgrass is tall. Most times, a little owl wouldn't have a prayer against a snake like that, but Gib was clever. Gib ran and hollered and got the King Snake so muddled in the head, he started eating his own tail. And he didn't stop till he had swallowed himself whole and disappeared off the face of the earth.

At least, they said, that was how Gib told the story. And there was no King Snake around, was there, so it must've been true. They all looked up to Gib. Gib was clever.

They chased around trees, through vines, across the soft ground, mad dashing one way, then another and another, and the air was crowded with yelling and laughing. Their games made no sense, chasing, hiding, seeking, rules always changing, one game blending into another. You could as easily chart a butterfly's course through a hurricane as understand their games.

They played until afternoon caught them and shadows took the island. The first of them was called home. "Tu-uuuuuudd!" Then, "Gib!" "Philomena, Lodemia!" A sharp mean voice screamed, "Clavis, get your butt home!"

The possum stayed where he was and Gib said, low, "Clavis, I think your dad's callin."

And the possum said, "Nobody tells Bevel what to do."

"Clavis, don't make me come lookin for you!" came the angry voice.

THE TALE OF THE SWAMP RAT

And the possum went, without another word.

Then *the mouse* got called and he was gone. One by one, they said good-bye and were gone. There was only Ossie. He went back, across the dry shore, out to the slough. He was filthy with dirt and mud when he crawled on the gator's shoulder and they set off through the cool dusk.

"You have a good time, boy?"

Ossie nodded, even as he nodded to sleep. His dreams were good that night. And each night after, each dream was a little bigger than the one before.

CHAPTER 15

GIVERS AND TAKERS

Some days the young ones went off exploring. The water was far enough gone, they could walk the swamp floor and find things that were hidden before. Gib the owl never joined these trips, for one reason or another—a chore, a visit, something would come up, always something.

Other days they spent trading stories. On this day, there was another game of chase. *the mouse* was It. Ossie and Gib were sharing a hiding place. When *the mouse* passed them a third time, Gib whispered, "Lookit him, lookit! He drives me crazy!" Ossie looked at *the mouse* with his small fretful face. "You feel sorry for him, for about five minutes. Then you want to slap him—but he's so little, you're afraid he'll break."

the mouse kept looking for them and not finding them and finally they got tired of waiting.

"Allright, look!" Gib called out. "Here's the deal! Some-body else is goin to be It!"

Then Ossie heard, "Hullo." The gopher turtle, again. "Name's Stubb." Again. The little turtle stayed there, smiling, until Ossie nodded back, hello. Then the turtle moved slowly off. The world came at Stubb one piece at a time, nothing con-nected to the next. It kept things simple, like that, and you had to half-envy him.

With a new game going, the little rat found a new hiding place. He was sure no one else knew of it. It was deep in the thick moon vine and a twisting narrow path led to the main stalk, where the place opened to a wide room. It reminded Ossie of the nest he'd been born in. In the days and weeks that followed, he hid there many times and was never found.

By midmorning, they were into the third or fourth game of the day. It was hard to know for sure. Ossie was rounding a turn in the path when he came on Johnny and his rat-friends. He stopped and one of them said to him, "Don't stand there like a fool, you fool, come on!" Another one shoved him and he went.

One of the rats was talking about a fight he'd been in and suddenly Ossie understood—they thought *he was one of them!* This wasn't good. This wasn't where he wanted to be. He had to find a way out of this.

Johnny stopped at the foot of a wide tree and said, "Let's go egg-dumpin."

The others were all for it, whatever it was. They started up the tree, all except Johnny and Ossie.

"What're you waitin on?" Johnny asked him.

Ossie shrugged.

"Get on up there," Johnny told him. Johnny wasn't older than Ossie, not much anyway. But Johnny looked twice Ossie's age. His body had grown faster than his brain had. He kept a pack of rat-friends around him always. They were smaller than he was and made him look even bigger. And they were all chewed up, one way or another, from the fighting they did. There were chipped teeth, missing teeth, half-tails, scabby torn ears. It was Ossie's scar that made them take him for one of their own.

He followed the rat-pack into the tree, there wasn't anything else he could do, and Johnny waited below. After they'd climbed a little higher, they headed out onto one moss-covered branch with a bird nest at the end.

There were several eggs in the nest and they pushed one out and off the branch. They watched it fall and break and they laughed. Johnny called up, "Now do another one!"

Ossie backed away, afraid and confused. He should stop them, should do something. They knocked the second egg from the nest and watched it fall. Then a third and a fourth and then they turned to Ossie.

"Go on, your turn."

Ossie took another step away.

"You want to get caught when the bird comes back? Move!"

But Ossie stayed where he was.

"What's wrong up there?" Johnny called. "Why's it takin so long?"

One of them pushed Ossie toward the nest.

"Hurry up, you fool."

"You're gettin Johnny mad, you fool."

Ossie looked and there was one egg left. "You knock it out, you fool, or we knock you out," a rat was saying, when there was a loud "Get away from there!"

It was Blue Pete, the kingfisher, and he was flying right at them. Ossie saw that Blue Pete knew him. The little rat moved away, into leafy branches, and the bird went after the others. He struck at them, chased them, then flew to the shattered eggs on the ground.

By now Ossie had climbed from the tree and run deep into the bushes, away from Johnny and his friends. He ran farther still. Uncle Will would find out what happened, sooner or later, Blue Pete would tell what happened. Ossie was sure of this.

He stayed there in the forest, alone and miserable, until night fell. Then, with the others gone, he found his way to the water. And he found the old alligator waiting.

CHAPTER 16

BEYOND A PARADISE TREE

Let me tell you a thing Will told me. Once he said to me, *I want to show you somethin important, Mole.* He always called me Mole, never *Little* Mole the way some of them do.

He told me about Ivory Bill, a bird who used to fly the swamp but flies it no more. Ivory Bill, the gator said, was a fine bird, big powerful bird who lived among the cypress for more years than even Will could remember. His wings were wide and his beak was strong enough to make holes in the hardest swamp tree. But then in the middle of one Summer day, the woodpecker Ivory Bill left our forest. And he did not come back. Will said, for all he knew, Ivory Bill would never come back. He was gone for good.

Look close, Mole, Will said to me, *and you'll see the hole he left in the swamp. Listen close, Mole, and you'll hear the song he isn't singin.*

Will told me this, though I am no more than a mole. And now I am telling you.

Sometimes I look. Sometimes I listen. I've seen the hole and heard the quiet and I understand that there are things in this swamp I will never understand.

Uncle Will was waiting the next morning, ready to take Ossie back to the island. They were halfway there when a sound cracked over the swamp. At first the little rat took it for thunder. But it wasn't. Will swam faster. There was a strange sound then, a hoot, but not any animal Ossie knew. Then another sharp pop echoed across the water.

Ossie looked behind him, up the slough, and he saw. There were two odd beasts such as he had never seen, tall thin things, bony-faced things. They moved through the water in a sort of hollow-out log called a Boat. These were Men, Will said, Poachers who kill gators for their hides.

One of the Men laughed wildly and the next moment, there were more shots. "Hoooey, we found him!" shouted the first. "We found him! It's him!"

"Whereat, Buford, whereat?"

"Listen to me, Dink! He's there, there, there!"

"I don't see nothin!"

"Open your eyes, Dink! Lookit the size! It's gotta be him!"

"Now I see, Buford! Now I see him! He's twenty feet, easy!"

"Twenty-five!"

"Must be a hunnert years old!"

"Six hunnert!"

More shots cracked, hitting around Ossie and Will. "Easy, Buford! Don't hurt the hide!" "But he's goin, Dink! We cain't lose him!"

Will moved faster, fast as Ossie had ever seen. "Hold on, boy," the gator said and he moved along the slough, through water hyacinth, around a low island full of palm, and then they were underwater. Even there Ossie heard the gunshots.

Will wouldn't stay under long. He came up looking for something, some place. The water was lower still and many channels were gone now. Where there had been wide pools, now were whole fields of things dry and dying. Will followed the full slough and the Men followed, too.

The gator found what he was looking for, a small hammock, a Paradise Tree at its edge. The Men were closer still. Will turned into a tight channel thick with tall grass. As he swam, the grass grew around them and the water stayed deep.

The Men in the Boat were coming, too.

Will moved quickly up the narrow stream, and Ossie worried. With the swamp so low, they might run out of water. Will would be an easy target on land. But the old alligator knew every piece of the swamp, wet and not. He knew what was beyond the Paradise Tree and he knew where water would be. Ossie held on. He could see the Men behind them, moving slower now. Sawgrass blades cut them as they pushed through.

Ossie heard them as Will made his way up this secret channel.

"What you figure we'd get for im?"

"More money than you could count, Dink!"

The voices were distant now.

"Man, we lost im!"

"Over there, Buford, over there!" one of them screamed, jumping.

"Whereat, Dink, whereat?"

"There! Alligator Flag!"

Poachers always look for Alligator Flag. They know it grows where the water is deep. Alligators hide where the water is deep. Poachers flush them out and kill them.

But Will had seen the Alligator Flag, too.

And Will had gone another way. They were in a browning field and the voices of the Men had faded. Farther on, the grasses gave way to cypress swamp. The water was gone here and trees grew one into another, a squeeze for a gator half Will's size. But he moved through without slowing. He could remember where every tree and root would be.

Another minute and the swamp opened and they came on a wide-edged pond. The little folk stopped their *skreee-skreeeee* as the gator swam in. Will paused and listened. There was nothing. He'd lost the Men.

From that unseen world, it started again. *Skreeeeeeeee-skreeeeeeee.*

Will slowly headed down the stream that fed the pond. As they came back to an open prairie, he stopped again, listened again.

Again there was nothing.

As they moved on, he told Ossie, "Those folk have been after me for a thousand years. They say they never saw a gator half so big as me and they prob'ly never did. They want to bring my skin out of the swamp. The one that does, he's gonna be a hero among em."

CHAPTER 17

BUTTERFLIES

The Summer days grew longer and still there was no rain. The water drew deeper into the earth. The land dried quickly in the heat and was like old bark under Ossie's feet. The air itself was brittle and scratched his insides. The light was dingy and yellow and so was everything it touched. The swamp had new smells. There was a stench of mud turned to dust, of plants dying in midday heat, an ugly smell of worse things to come.

Uncle Will took the little rat to the island and the young ones were trying to get a game started. But the possum was late getting there. When he finally showed up, Gib the owl said, "Why're you always late, Clavis?"

"Clavis, who's Clavis?" said the possum Clavis. "I am El-wood."

"Look," Gib said, "here's the deal. Elwood, you tell Clavis it's his turn to be It."

"I was It the last three times!" the possum yelled.

"YOU WERE NOT!" Lodemia said back.

"Foot! Here we go again," said the little crabby rat.

They all started in then, yelling and screaming.

"Well, what about him?" another rat said. "The new rat."

"Yeah, what about *him*?" said some of the others. "He's never been It."

"We can't make him It," said Tudd the armadillo.

"Why—why—why not?" *the mouse* wanted to know.

"Because he doesn't talk!" Tudd answered.

"Doesn't or can't?"

"Can't or don't want to?"

"Don't want to or don't like to?"

"Does he know how?"

"Foot!"

"Oh, leave him alone," came another voice, a new voice.

Ossie looked. He looked twice. He looked a third time. Yeah. It was. It was her. A little older, but her. The girl-rat he'd seen so long ago. And only that once. As beautiful as he remembered. Or maybe a little more.

"Allright, look," Gib said, "here's the deal. I'll be It!"

And he was. And the game, at last, began. They went running off into that long Summer day, but Ossie didn't run with them. He stayed behind. Just himself with the girl. He stood there, silent, embarrassed, but he managed a smile.

And she smiled back. And that was good.

She said, "Hi."

And he looked at the ground.

"My name's Emma," she said.

And Ossie kept looking at the ground. He was shaking, and he hoped she couldn't tell. He felt her looking at him, half-remembering.

"Do I know you?" she asked.

He shook his head, no.

"We haven't met?"

He shook his head again.

"Seems I know you. From somewhere. Somehow."

He wanted to say yes, of course, you remember it, too. But then there was a far-off call. "Emma!"

"Gotta go," she said and was gone. She stopped once, quickly, to call "Bye," and that was it.

And Ossie said, "Butterflies."

That's how it happened. Just like that, it happened. He had a voice. He said the first word he'd said and no one was there to hear it. Not a soul.

Well, there was one. A little under the ground, there was me. I heard it. *Butterflies,* he said, clear as day. You can take my word on this.

I don't know what it was about the girl, but it was something. She was the one who let him find his voice. Now, that one little word was all he said. But it was a start. Ossie sat there for a time, going over the short moments in his head.

Then he ran and joined the game and he wasn't the same rat he'd been.

It was First Dark when Ossie met Will at the shore. The little rat was filthy with mud and he crawled on the gator's shoulder. As Will made his way down the channel, he said, "Looks like you had a big day."

"Yeah, Uncle Will," the swamp rat said. "I did."

It stopped the gator, that. He drifted awhile.

Then he said, "Oh."

And they moved on into the night.

"You don't say."

CHAPTER 18

ANOTHER PROPHECY

There is a thing that happens to trees. It happens to big trees, oak and cypress. It begins, like the tree, as a tiny seed. I guess a bird drops the seed. Then maybe it grows. Maybe it doesn't. If it grows, it grows into a vine.

The vine moves up the tree and wraps around, around it. The vine grows back over itself, into itself, crossing, again, again. It grows broader, bigger, thicker. It covers the tree and holds it in a murdering grip and they call it Strangler Fig. In time the tree dies. In time it falls. In time it rots away. And the Strangler Fig stays. There's nothing left but hollow space where the tree had been. And a vine with nothing left to strangle.

It was in such a tree, a strangling tree, that the Prophet Bubba sat and watched folk gather. They brought fish. Bubba waited for a good crowd to show up. Then he said, loud enough to scare children and weakhearted types, "LISTEN TO ME!"

They listened.

"There ain't no drought in this swamp."

A wordless wave passed over the crowd. *Ain't no drought? What's he mean? Hasn't been this dry in a loooooong time,* they thought but didn't say.

Bubba went on, "There'd be water ever'where weren't it not for the gopher turtle!"

I don't know what it was about that bird. There was something inside him, some grain of dirt wearing at his soul. When folk were calmed down, he had to rile them up. When things were quiet, he had to make some noise. When that thing itched him, he had to scratch.

No gopher turtles were there to hear Bubba and that was good.

None of the swamp folk said anything. None of them knew what to say. They were too confused. Gopher turtles weren't bad folk, were they? They burrowed holes in the ground and bothered no one. Some even shared their homes with the homeless. How could the Prophet Bubba say this was the fault of the turtles?

He explained. "The gophers have dug too many burrows. The water is drainin into their holes. The whole blasted swamp is drainin into their holes! Y'all shoulda seen this by now! I oughtn't to have to tell y'all this!"

No word rose from the crowd. No one had given this any thought. An old blind possum and an elder raccoon whispered over it.

"Reckon it might be?" the raccoon asked.

"If Bubba says it is, it is," the possum whispered back. "Everythin the Prophet says is so, is so. Like the rabbit with a left-lopped ear, you remember."

And the raccoon did remember. "Yes, yes."

A year ago, Bubba warned that if a young rabbit came to the swamp and his left ear was bent, there would be trouble. His fur would be brown-gray, dotted with white. If this rabbit showed up before the next full moon, it would be the beginning of a bad time. The days would grow cold, colder than anyone had known. This would last a week. Then bees would swarm in billowing clouds, so thick the sun would fade behind them. They would descend on the islands and attack every living creature. They would not leave until a great wind from the east blew them from the swamp. But then it would be too late. The damage would be done. Folk would suffer.

But they were lucky. No such rabbit showed up. They were spared the horror. It was no less than a Miracle.

No one doubted the Prophet Bubba this time either. When he said they could save themselves, they listened. Bubba said they'd have to find all the gopher-turtle holes and fill them in.

If as much as one hole was missed, the Prophet warned—even one hole!—the water would keep draining. They'd have to wait for rain to fill the swamp again.

The swamp folk knew there was no choice. They set right to work.

As for the gopher turtles, their lives were miserable now. When folk came around filling their burrows, they could not understand. Every time a turtle tried to dig a new hole, some-body came along and filled it.

When Preacher caught wind of what was happening, he tried to stop it. "Don't go causin them turtles grief and what-all," he said. "Those folk're blameless!"

But the swamp folk could not ignore the Prophet's prophecy. Every time a gopher turtle dug a new home, it was filled in with dirt. After a while, the turtles got tired of it. They got up and left the swamp, most of them.

Still, the water only got lower. Somewhere out there, the swamp folk knew, was a burrow they had missed.

GRANDMOTHER EARLIE

Here is a thing Will told Ossie. "All shadows are the same and that's the Secret of Life." The shadow a sparrow makes is no different from a bear's. A hundred-foot oak and a tangle of pokeweed each shade the earth, one same as the other. Everyone who crosses the face of the swamp casts a shadow and all shadows are made of the same stuff. The swamp doesn't care whose shadow is whose. The swamp doesn't care one whit. The swamp has bigger things on its mind. This is the Secret of Life, but don't tell anyone.

Gib was saying, "Look. Here's the deal. It's—"

"Wait." The possum stopped him there. "Jasper the Great can see the future before it happens. Jasper the Great can read your very mind. You are goin to say that Clavis is now It."

"Yeah," said Gib, "that's exactly what I was goin to say."

"Wooo," said one of the Rat-Brothers, "he *can* see the future!"

"And I bet," Gib went on, "that Jasper the Great knows I'm goin to say him and Clavis are one in the same."

"Jasper knows all."

"So he knows I'm goin to say it's Jasper's turn, same as it's Clavis's."

"Aw, come on," whined Clavis, "you're always sayin I'm It! I'm not It!"

"You are, too!"

"I am not!"

"Foot!" said the crabby rat.

"Uh, excuse me, but I—I—I believe it actually is your turn," said *the mouse.*

"See," said Gib, "even *the mouse* says so, in his own irritatin way."

"Um, thank you."

"It ain't my turn!" shouted Jasper. Clavis.

"It is!"

"Ain't!"

"Is!" yelled Gib.

"Ain't!" Clavis yelled back. "You don't believe me, ask him."

"Ask who?"

"Ask what's-his-name," and Clavis looked at Ossie.

And the swamp rat said, "Ossie."

"Yeah," said Clavis, "ask Ossie."

For one short second, they didn't think anything about it. But the next second, Philomena whispered to Gib, "Did he say somethin?"

Tudd answered, but he answered to himself.

"What he said was his name's Ossie," the armadillo muttered, "and that's somethin we didn't know before," Tudd was telling himself, "cause he's never talked before."

The swamp rat turned when he heard, "Hullo. Name's Stubb."

"I'm Ossie," the rat said.

"Hullo, Ossie," said Stubb.

And now the others were stepping close, saying, "Hi, Ossie," and he said "Hi" to them.

And the game began and Ossie was It.

With each day, Ossie found more words. And the more words he let out, the more new ones came to take their place.

In the middle of their play that morning, Ossie raced up the dry shore and around a stand of palms and suddenly there was Emma. He nearly ran into her.

"Hello," he said.

She said, "Hi."

He said, "My," and he caught some breath and said, "name," and he caught some more and said, "is," and then, "Ossie."

"Hello, Ossie," is what she said back.

Then he said, "You're Emma," like maybe she didn't know.

She smiled and told him, "Yeah, I am." Her eyes were gray and green and brown and always changing, and if he looked away there was no telling what he might miss.

It was a quiet moment and it went on too long. Ossie felt a nauseous knot somewhere in the bottom of his stomach. The silence scared him and his throat started twisting into tight little knots. If he talked, the words might come out as strangled squeaks.

But no. He wasn't going to let that happen, not this time.

And, in a jumble of words, he told her who he was and where he lived and Preacher, Rufus, the Seminole, the—but now he was talking *too much,* so he shut up.

Just then a strong wind blew past, turning every leaf of every tree. A lone little butterfly was caught in the wind and sent blowing by, helpless. *"The wind, the wind! I am nothin in the face of the wind!"* it screamed, minute but dramatic. They watched as the butterfly was carried over the dry scabby land and on toward the rise of the next distant island. *"I surrender my fate to the wind! The wind . . . ! The wind . . . !"*

Ossie said, abruptly, "We saw butterflies once."

There. He saw it in her face. She didn't know what he was talking about.

"We what . . . ?" she said.

He felt his throat twisting again. He said, "Nothin. I mean, I was talkin to myself."

She said, "Oh. Yeah. Allright." Then she said, looking toward the far island, "I think my great-great-grandmother lives over there. I've never met her. Her name is Earlie."

"Do you want to go?" Ossie asked and quickly. "The water's gone. We could walk."

She wanted to go, very much, so they went. And as they went, Ossie thought this: There was really no telling what might be over there. Mr. Took or some worse thing he hadn't even thought of. This could be a very dangerous journey.

Then again, it might turn out well.

It might or it might not.

If it wasn't one, it'd be the other.

He'd find out soon.

The land here was flat and open. Ossie worried, there was nothing to hide them from hawks. "We better hurry," he said and they did, until they were safe in the cover of the new island.

Neither of them saw who *was* watching. Over in a vine patch, one of Johnny's rat-gang was sniffing around. He saw them. He sat very still. When Emma and Ossie were on the other island, he went running.

"Do you know the way?" Ossie asked Emma.

"No," she said, "but you and me can find it." Soon they came across a pig frog and Emma asked if he knew Earlie.

The frog chewed on it a while and said, "Oh!" And then he said, "You're talkin bout *Old Earlie*!"

Emma nodded, she guessed that was right.

"Assumin she's still livin. Old Earlie is the oldest rat in the swamp."

The pig frog thought there was a rat-lodge somewhere on the far side of the island. She lived over there, is what he thought.

But soon a red squirrel pointed them on a different path. "Mean Old Earlie lives *that* way." And the squirrel added, "You know she's twicet as old as any rat ever was, and at least twicet as mean."

A wood duck sent them east. "They say she's almost as old as Old Uncle Will and near as mean as Mr. Took."

The farther they went, the older and meaner Old Earlie got.

At last they were across the island and found the nest and Ossie was wishing he'd never suggested this. The lodge was big, overpowering. It was dark and had been around a long time. Just inside, they came on a rat who told them about the small chamber where Old Earlie stayed, never leaving.

Emma and Ossie passed sleeping quarters, storage rooms, and finally found her far in the belly of the lodge, deep in the corner of a shadowy room. She didn't see them at first, didn't know they were there. Her fur was thin and white, her teeth worn away to nothing, her eyes clouded from watching a lot of days go by. Ossie couldn't tell how old she was, only that she was old. Very old.

Suddenly she saw them. "Who're y'all!?" she screamed. "What're y'all doin here!?"

Ossie felt his heart stop working and waited for it to start again. Emma flattened herself against the far wall, too scared to move. "It's . . . me, Emma—" she started to say.

But the old rat didn't want to hear. She was screaming at them again. "Get out now! Get out!"

Ossie was ready to go. Those others had been wrong. Old Earlie was a lot older and a lot meaner. They were getting out when Old Earlie said, "Who're y'all anyway?"

Emma said, "Em—"

And Earlie said, "You ain't Emma? Huh?"

Emma nodded, she was.

"My own great-great-granddaughter Emma?"

Emma nodded again.

Old Earlie smiled now. "Emma," she said. "Imagine. Haven't seen you since you were a baby. But you look juuuu-uuust like your mother! Not like your father, the funny-lookin coot." The smile changed the old rat's face and made it younger. Ossie's eyes were getting more used to the dark and he was seeing that Old Earlie really wasn't that old. Not as old as she acted. She wasn't screaming now and her voice was a surprise, young and almost happy. There was nothing mean in it. Emma took a step closer and Ossie waited in a shadow.

Words poured out of Old Earlie, hardly a break between them. "Isn't it awful, us livin on different islands? We never get to see each other, not with all that distance. It's awful, just awful!" Old Earlie hurried over to kiss Emma. "I used to hear about you all the time! The birds would bring word back. They'd tell the moles and the moles would tell me."

Emma tried to speak again, but her great-great-grandmother talked right over her. Ossie saw, and Emma, too, that the old rat was deaf. She heard nothing they said. She filled the silence in her head with the echo of her own voice. In that same silence, everyone else heard meanness.

"Well, I *think* those birds were tellin the moles. Sometimes I wonder. I wonder do moles overhear a little and make up the rest. You know how moles are. But then it stopped, I don't know how long ago. It just stopped. Word stopped comin like that. I never heard any more from em."

Ossie hadn't been in a rat-lodge in a long time, not since his own. He remembered the smells and thought about the snake. Old Earlie kept talking an hour or more, no pauses even to breathe. She talked about family, this uncle, that cousin, and the talk had no meaning for Ossie. But he liked listening to Emma listen.

There was nothing he didn't like about Emma. He didn't know why. But he did know this. When he was around her, things seemed worth doing, or trying, and what was wrong with that?

• • •

THE TALE OF THE SWAMP RAT

He thought Old Earlie had forgotten him, until she said, "Who's your friend there, hidin in shadow?"

Ossie stayed where he was.

"Come on," Emma said.

He moved closer. Old Earlie stared hard and asked, "You kin to those folk the snake got? You look like one of em. I knew those folk, and you look like one of em."

Ossie jumped. He hadn't expected this. There was nothing left of his family but dim memory and each day less of that. Now here was Old Earlie, clearing a path to them.

"We heard what happened to y'all," she said, quiet, "even here, we heard what happened. Terrible thing." And she added, "Little Mole told us."

Ossie saw that Emma knew nothing of it.

"I knew some of your folk. You had a grandfather, maybe great-great-great. He lived here. I knew him. He was famous, but you know all about him."

Ossie shook his head, no.

"Go on! Sure you heard about *him*!"

But Ossie shook his head, no, again.

"Poor Elmo, he was a hero among swamp rats. Larger than life, more or less. I was little back then. It was Summer, terrible time, dry as this and worse. Heat lightnin all day. Then, all the sudden, there was Wildfire in the grass. One second ever'thin was allright, the next there it was. Wherever we went, there was fire. East, north, one big circle squeezin tight.

"Folk were runnin ever'way but the right way. Not just swamp rats, you unnerstan, but all folk. Raccoon, possum, bear, even gators. Ever'body was so addled from fear, they didn't know what to do.

"Then somebody remembered. There was one rat we could

turn to. He'd proved hisself brave many times. He fought snakes, chased raccoons off from the lodge. A fine specimen! He could help us out of that mess.

"His name was Elmer.

"You can imagine how it was, a time like that. Folks runnin, screamin, hollerin, all confusion. They were callin for Elmer, but it was Poor Elmo who said, 'Whut?' That's how he got took for a hero. Elmer, Elmo, awful close. See, it was just a misunnerstandin. Your trice-great-granddaddy was a decent soul, but he was nothin to look at. Scrawny, scrunched over, bony old coot, no chin you'd notice. Poor Elmo was no Elmer. But the mistake was made, and it stayed made.

"Ever'body was countin on him. Poor Elmo had no hint how a hero acts, din't know what-all steps were involved. He only knew it had to be flashy and get folks' attention.

"He climbed the tallest pine he could find—even bein scared of high places like he was! He kept climbin that tree—even as it was startin to burn—and from up top, he saw a break in the flames. He found us a path out! It wasn't much, he said, and closin up fast. We'd have to go quick.

"Some of the other folk din't believe him. Deer and bear and big folk like that. 'You ain't but a swamp rat and a scrawny one, too!' they said. 'Why should we listen to you?' Some of em din't listen. But us rats did.

"He got us together and showed us the way. Times, he seemed to walk us straight into flame, but it turned out right somehow. He took us clear to Big Cypress and past. We were safe there. Lucky thing, rain come shortly and chased off the fire.

"We'd've burnt up, 'tweren't for Poor Elmo. Lot of folk *din't* make it, but not one swamp rat was hurt that day."

Emma listened to the story as close as Ossie.

"I was a child, but I remember like it was this mornin. Poor Elmo was a hero to us all. There were songs about him—but they never caught on. Truth is, the songs weren't *real* good. I think it was cause of that name. You try rhymin Elmo."

She told him about his parents. One Winter, with the swamp dry, the families of his mother and father came to this island. Ossie's folk met right around here.

His father was always curious and one day he took Ossie's mother off exploring. It was early Spring and they'd been gone half a day when a storm blew in out of nowhere. No one saw it coming, as bad as it was. Turned into a five-day flooder and half a season's rain fell in less than a week. The swamp filled deep, so high it covered some islands altogether.

Nobody knew what happened to Ossie's parents. Folk figured they'd been caught in the fast-rising water. Folk figured the mangroves took them. Folk always figured the worst.

It was months later when somebody heard from a mole who heard from a bird that the rats were safe. They'd made it to an island down south and were living there. They'd started a family already.

Old Earlie stopped now. She was tired. Emma nodded to Ossie, they should leave. He started out with her, but stopped when he heard, "You're the spittin image of Hitch."

Ossie turned around and looked at her. She thought he hadn't heard.

"Hitch, I said. Hitch. Your father."

It was late when they got to the island. Ossie said good-bye to Emma and went to find the others. "Hullo," the turtle said. "Name's Stubb."

The little rat nodded and smiled, once again. "I'm Ossie," he said.

They were gathered on the shore, worn out, Gib, Tudd, Clavis, the rest. "Where were you hidin, Ossie?" "We looked ever'where!" "Three times!"

He was wondering whether to tell them, when someone yelled, "HEY!"

And, "YOU!"

Johnny was there with his rat-gang.

"Get here right now!"

Ossie stayed where he was and *the mouse* said to Johnny, "I really don't think it—it—it's polite talkin to him in that—well, talkin to him that way." Johnny paid *the mouse* no mind at all.

"I'm waitin!"

"And I'm thinkin maybe," Tudd whispered to Ossie, "you ought to run."

"We'll slow him down," Philomena the quail added, quiet.

But Ossie didn't go. Johnny came closer, his rat-gang just behind him. There was something strange about Johnny's friends and Ossie saw what it was: You never knew how many there were. Even when you looked, you didn't know. Even when you counted, you didn't know. There were three, four, maybe five, maybe less. One was too much like the other. They were only a pack.

Ossie saw one of them whisper to Johnny, "That's him, it's him, I seen him, I did."

Johnny pushed close. "Were you talkin to her?"

"To who?" Ossie asked, a squeak.

"Emma."

Ossie could tell, Johnny was enjoying himself. He liked these chances to bully somebody. He never missed one.

The other rat nodded. "If he says no, he's lyin! I seen em! I was there! They went off together! Off the island! I seen em!"

Johnny said, slow, mean, "Is that true?"

Gib, Tudd, Clavis, and the others—they all hated Johnny, just now. And Johnny knew it, you could tell. Johnny liked it. Johnny loved it, you could tell. He wouldn't have traded places with anybody, not just now.

"I asked, is it true?" Johnny said, slower, meaner.

"Yes," Ossie finally answered.

Tudd was talking to himself again.

"That's why we couldn't find him, cause he wasn't even here," the armadillo was telling himself, "so I guess we didn't make the rules plain. He's gotta be here if we're gonna find him," and he plotted and he planned, "so next time, we got to lay out the rules better."

"I don't want you around my sister," Johnny was saying. "You unnerstan what I'm tellin you?"

And there it was. There was something for you. Johnny, Emma. Emma, Johnny. Brother, Sister. There was something Ossie could live without.

The little rat turned to Johnny and said, "No."

It wasn't what Johnny wanted to hear, not quite. Words poured, "No what? you don't got it? what's not to get? tell me what you don't get! you stay away, that's all!"

And Ossie said, "No," again. (Johnny heard his rat-gang muttering and he squirmed. He was as afraid of them as they were of him.)

Johnny jumped at Ossie.

But Ossie fought, and hard, and Johnny wasn't ready for it. They bit, tumbled, twisted. Johnny's rat-gang saw how bad it was and pulled back into the swamp forest, very quiet. The fight kept on and on, worse and worse. Ossie was not going to give up.

Johnny was dirty, bleeding, a front tooth broken out. Ossie jumped into him, headfirst, and Johnny went rolling. And he rolled right into a pool of standing water, splashing, coughing. It was the foul water Ossie had seen days before and it was fouler now.

The big rat crawled out and he dripped with stinking muck, his fur was thick with the stench of rotted fish and plants turned to brown filth. Gib and the rest had never seen Johnny look like this. Johnny had never looked like this. It might take a month to wear that smell off.

"Goooooooood Loooooord," said Tudd, long and quiet.

And then Johnny's mother saw him.

In the swamp they still talk about what happened next. It started with loud screams and wild curses, Johnny's mother running at him, snapping his ears, chasing him, nipping him, yelling, all the way home, *"Look at you! Look! You're a mess! I've warned you! Why have you done this to me!"*

The sound of his mother's screams rained over the swamp for hours, not letting up except as she caught her breath. (Ossie worried what Emma would think, but when she saw him next, she only said, "It was about time.")

Gib and Tudd and the rest were glad. Johnny wouldn't bother them for a while. He wouldn't bother *anybody* for a while. It takes time to live down a thing like that, when your mother lets into you like that. Ossie turned to go and he found Blue Pete, on a tree stump, watching. The kingfisher had seen the whole thing. He said, "How you feelin, little fellow? You okay?"

Ossie said, "Yes."

Blue Pete nodded. "Good, good, that's good," then flew into the forest.

Ossie saw Uncle Will swimming to the island and went to meet him.

CHAPTER 20

WILL'S SECOND DREAM

The others were off spreading the news about Johnny as Ossie waited for Will. Nine dragonflies moved above him and talked among themselves. And Ossie heard them. *"That's the one,"* said one.

"The one who beat the livin daylights outta the bully," said another.

"But who is he, that's what I want to know, who is he?!" screeched the third, high-strung.

"He's the one Will saved," said the fourth.

"The one with no family," said the fifth.

"Mr. Took found the nest," added the sixth.

"Mr. Took got them all," said the seventh.

"The mangroves," said the eighth, *"have them now."*

"All but that one," the ninth said.

• • •

Will came and they went heading into the swamp, but in a moment they stopped. Ossie saw, ahead in the near-distance, a large hammock. There was a gator mound on it and the Gator-Mother watched her newborn children crawl from nest to water. A couple of raccoons sat in a tree, waiting, watching. Hawk was circling the sky, watching, waiting. A lean young alligator lay in the water, waiting, watching. If a baby strayed off, these folk would be ready to get them. Even another alligator would eat one if he could.

It isn't an easy world for a gator, just-born. It's a harder world than you might think.

Uncle Will made a loud move to let Hawk and the gator and the raccoons know he was there. Then he settled in the water to watch. Hawk drifted toward a cloud, the raccoons backed off into the forest, the young gator swam up a narrow slough. The babies would be safe today. Uncle Will could make these things happen, and just from the way he looked.

Ossie wondered why things were the way they were. "Why're the big ones," he asked, "always pickin on the little ones? Why's it always like that?"

"Isn't always," Will answered. "In time, the weak grow strong," he said. "In time, the strong grow weak." It was First Dark now and the gator started telling Ossie another of his Dreams. And it was this.

Fifteen long Centuries before the Seminole came, there were others here. There were Indians low in the Swamp and they were the Calusa. They built houses and whole cities and grew into a great tribe, their Power spreadin wide. With shells from the sea, they made jewelry to decorate themselves. With Wood from the forests, they carved masks to cover their faces for dance and celebration. They built long low Boats to move themselves across the Water.

They were a fierce tribe and made Slaves of others. They fought many Fights. They won many Victories.

Centuries came and went and one day big ships from a world across the sea brought strange White Men to the Swamp. And the Calusa were there. At times they met in peace, at times they fought.

The Calusa were a great tribe, a fierce tribe. They fought many Fights and won many Victories. Sometimes they made Slaves of the White Man.

But all things must change, that is the Way. More years came and went and the Calusa were great and fierce no longer.

Then one day, they were gone. They were gone from their houses, from their cities, from the Swamp, from the Earth. As great as they were, as fierce as they fought, they were gone.

They could not Save themselves from Time.

I don't know what became of em. Some say they moved deeper in the Swamp and came to be part of other tribes. I can only tell you the Calusa have gone. No one knows what happened, no one ever will.

This is one of the Secrets the Swamp keeps for its own.

CHAPTER 21

A SECRET AMONG DRAGONFLIES

*The full Song of the Swamp goes on with no end,
and takes many voices to sing it.*

—a swamp saying

They set out early for the island, sun barely up. Will watched the water drop through the swamp and Ossie thought of Emma. They rounded the bending slough and it widened to a pool of water hyacinth, purple-blue flowers rattling in a morning breeze. It was a beautiful place, a perfect place. But no matter how many times they passed this way, and they *often* did, Ossie always forgot this part of the journey. Each time they came on the hyacinth field, this piece of the world was new to him.

As they went through the swamp, a dragonfly hung in the air beside Ossie and looked at him, once, twice, then flew off into a forest. It reminded the little rat of things the dragon-flies had whispered the day before.

"Uncle Will," he asked, "what's it mean when the mangroves take you?"

"It means you're done, boy," Will told him. "It means you pass on, means you die."

Ossie only nodded.

"The swamp is a river of water, wide and pure, and it flows to the mangroves. The walkin tree, they call em. Grows right in the air, roots danglin to reach water."

Ossie watched the dawning sun and tried to picture this place with trees grown from the air and roots reaching for water. But he could not.

"When you pass on," Will was saying, "the river floats you to the mangroves. It floats you into those roots and nobody sees you again."

"But what's on the other side?"

"Don't know. Never been there. Birds say there's a whole ocean and more worlds past. But that's birds talkin."

After a longer while Will said, "S'pose it doesn't much matter what's on the other side. Once the mangroves take you, you're not comin back."

Emma's Island was still on the horizon. "Your friends won't be up just yet," Will said. "We'll wait here." The rising sun had only found the top of the hammock trees. The rest lay deep in cold shadow.

Ossie suddenly said, "We've gone a lot of places, Uncle Will."

"We'll go more."

"There's one place I want to see. I want to see where I was born."

"Yeah," Will said, "reckon you will, in time." Because time, Will knew, would grow vines over the wrecked home and time would wear away the scent of his family.

"I want to go there," Ossie said. "I'd like to go. Could we go now?"

It was a little while before Uncle Will said, "If you want," and they went.

It only took a short time. Ossie thought it would be days from here, weeks, maybe more. But it wasn't far, just south of Emma's Island. The water had drawn away from the hammock and Will crawled onto land growing warm in the early sun.

Ossie jumped down, but didn't go farther.

"Not a big place," Will said. "S'pose you'll find your own way."

"S'pose."

Ossie headed into the forest and the old alligator waited on the shore.

Once or twice, he thought about turning back. But he'd come this far and he kept going.

Memories glanced around his head, but so briefly, he was barely sure they were his own. That path—he once got lost down there, didn't he? And that cabbage palm, he fell out of it once. That bush, he'd eaten a half-bad berry off it, long ago. And past the twisted vines—he got lost there, too, didn't he? Yes, he knew this place. A little farther on, he saw a tree choked by Strangler Fig. Then, a field of silk grass. Beyond a giant fern, that's where his house would be. He knew this.

As he crawled under the fern, grown big and snarled, he found it.

It wasn't rotting, wasn't crumbling. A new rat-family had taken it over. Whatever the snake had done, they had fixed. The place was bigger, nicer. There must have been a dozen children playing around it. The Rat-Mother and Rat-Father added twigs to the lodge, making it bigger still. It was theirs now.

Ossie soon left.

They went to Emma's Island after that and everyone was already playing. "Where were you?" Emma asked him.

"Off somewhere," he mumbled, "with Uncle Will."

"So it's true? You know that old gator? You're friends with him?" Ossie nodded. "What a thing that must be," she said, quiet, to herself.

The next day Ossie set it up for her to meet Will.

Ossie and Emma carefully made their way to a hidden shore. Will was waiting and the two little rats crawled on. Emma's family, her parents, even their friends could never know about this.

Will swam through what water was still left to the swamp.

He took them out that day, and several days after. He took them to the house where the Seminole had lived, they met Preacher, saw the Piney Wood. They saw the ibis rookery, still loud and full.

One day they went to the channel where Rufus swam and spent a long afternoon there. The manatee laughed and told his stories and Ossie and Emma climbed onto cypress knees and listened. One tale he told was this.

The Watchers' Tale

Way back when, before anybody thought to keep track of time, there were strange folk wanderin the swamp. And one of the strangest was called Estenco. He looked a little like raccoon and a little like wood stork and somethin like garfish, around the eyes anyway. The Estenco were decent folk, least at the start. They had brains as good as you or me. But before long, their attitudes went bad. These folk thought they had the world figured out. They were right and nobody else was.

The Estenco would just sit in the shade of the cypress trees, stuffin food in their faces and starin into space, hour after day after week. If they ever said a thing, it was likely nasty.

"Come on, Estenco, let's go play," the turtles might call.

And the Estenco would grunt, "Got better things to do."

And the turtles might ask, "Things like what?"

"Like what I'm doin," the Estenco would grunt back.

In time, ever'body else in the swamp started callin em The Watchers—cause that's all they ever did. They watched. And they watched and they watched.

Time kept goin, and The Watchers got lazier and still lazier. And then they got lazier. Their stomachs grew bigger and their brains, gettin no use at all, grew smaller.

You'd ask em somethin and they'd grunt, "Huh," cause *huh* was about the only word left to em. Then they lost that one, too.

But The Watchers kept eatin and starin, even after their brains went to dust. They got so lazy, they stopped movin altogether. They would eat whatever weeds were growin close to em. Then they'd wait for new weeds to grow back.

Then came a Dry Time and the weeds didn't grow back. The other swamp folk had to search and search for food. But The Watchers were too lazy to bother. And they didn't have brains to know what was wrong.

So they just ceased to be, right where they were sittin, there in the shade of the cypress trees, watchin. It was a while before anybody noticed, cause a dead Watcher and a livin one weren't that different.

Soon, their bodies turned hard like cypress and the wind and the rain smoothed the edges off em. When the water came back, it rose up around em.

Those knobby things you see in the swamp, that's all that's left of The Watchers. Folk call em cypress knees.

And Rufus said, "Like the ones you're sittin on now," and Emma and Ossie jumped off them.

Over the next days, Will took them to the island with the Paradise Tree, to the cypress forest where they listened to Preacher's stories-without-end. They went to the field of hyacinth, to the wide prairies where they heard Panther's distant cry. Emma had never known such places were here and so close. They saw more and still more.

They were moving across a grassy plain and another day was ending. Ossie thought, even then, that these might be the best times he'd ever know. He tried to force a memory of it. The sun was setting and they listened.

This swamp, our swamp, can be a place of endless beauty, one moment giving way to the next and leaving it all new again. A fresh wind blew over Ossie and he closed his eyes, afraid of waking from a dream.

CHAPTER 22
STUBB

I ask you. How could they not see? How could they not notice?

Still, they didn't see. They didn't notice. But don't ask me how.

They were changing, all of them, right in front of their own eyes. The quail Lodemia was small and round one day and the next she was taller, leaner. Her sister Philomena went home one afternoon tripping and falling over her own feet and came back the next morning prancing, light-footed. The Rat-Brothers grew lean, strong, self-sure. Emma, well, Emma grew more remarkable in every way. Gib the owl looked more and more like the son of his father and the turtle Stubb was Stubb, but bigger and bigger. They were growing, changing, all of them. But they never noticed it, the crazy endless dance they were dancing.

• • •

This morning, the swamp rat had just got to the island when he heard the others calling, "Stubb! *Stuuuubb!*" Nobody could find the gopher turtle. They had looked everywhere and he was nowhere. They set off searching again.

They finally found him with his family, standing, staring at a pile of dirt.

"Hullo," the turtle said to Ossie. "Name's Stubb."

"Ossie," the swamp rat said.

"What's that?" the little owl Gib asked, a whisper, as he stared at the pile of dirt.

"Pile of dirt," said Stubb.

"Allright," said Gib. "And what else is it?"

"Used to be home." Their burrow had been filled in, for a third time.

"Well," said Stubb. "Well, well," said his father. "Well, well, well," his mother added to that. (They got along fine, Stubb's family.)

Stubb said they'd left for breakfast. When they came back, there was this where the house had been. A pile of dirt. Ossie remembered what Preacher told him of Bubba's prophecy, how he said all the turtle burrows should be filled.

"Foot!" said the unhappy rat. "They had no right doin that!"

"Occurs to me," Stubb's father was saying, and slowly, "maybe we aren't wanted here. Maybe we ought to find somewhere else to live."

A while went by before Stubb's mother said, "That's right," and nothing more.

"Myrna's got kin over to Devil's Garden."

And Myrna, the Turtle-Mother, said, "That's right."

"Um, excuse me, but isn't that—that—that a long way off?" asked *the mouse,* timid. He'd heard a crow talk about the place. It was off past the edge of the swamp, beyond the Big Cypress.

"That's right," said the mother.

"Things might be better there," the Turtle-Father was saying now.

"Things won't be worse," Myrna added.

That was how it would be. Stubb would leave. They were already saying good-bye, the family gathering itself.

Tudd was muttering and mumbling. Tudd liked things thought-out before they happened and things like this— unexpected, unreasonable things—could throw him off for days.

"No, wait a minute," said Ossie. "I don't think you have to go."

The turtles turned to look, the whole family.

Ossie went on, "We'll get you another house, here, a new one."

The Turtle-Father only shook his head. "Son, it'd just happen again. Same as this. Somebody'd come along and fill it in."

"Not if it was hidden," Ossie said. "I know a place. Nobody'll ever find you there."

The Turtle-Father shook his head again. And in time he said, "Used to be, I was patient as a buzzard. Used to be, I wouldn't mind makin a house agin and agin. But, son, I've dug three houses this week. All of em got filled in. I'm bone-tired."

Ossie said, "We'll make it for you."

And they did. Ossie took his friends to the moon vine, his old hiding place, and led them up the confused path to the wide opening in the center. And there they began to work. Uncle Will had shown Ossie how to dig; the little owl Gib had known how to burrow the minute he was born; and Tudd's armadillo claws moved easily through the loose soil. The rats and the Quail-Sisters helped, *the mouse* did what he could, and Clavis the possum slept.

They built it hidden deep in the moon vine, a nice burrow, well-made and thought-out. The entrance angled, sloping, down deep. Off this, there were a half-dozen sleeping rooms, a big place for them to gather, a wide low storage chamber, each room laid out with care and reason. The floors and walls were trod smooth, no loose dirt or pebbles. Root ends were cut back, flush with the walls and ceilings.

Once, as he was taking some cut roots from the tunnel, Ossie felt something in the morning air. He sensed something, something not right.

He paused, trying to understand. It was a smell—no, the memory of a smell. A sharp bitter smell.

And Ossie knew. He knew it was the smell of a snake, a large one, a rattlesnake. The scent was old, yet it still hung to the air. Ossie was certain, Mr. Took had been here once. Perhaps it had been a season ago, maybe two, but Mr. Took had crossed this land. Ossie was certain of that.

But the snake was not here now and had not been for a long time. Ossie was certain of that, too. The swamp rat went back to the tunnel and joined the others.

Ossie worked hardest of them all. He threw himself into it

and went at it with everything he had. At day's end, he wondered why his paws were blistered, his shoulder burning sore, his whole self so completely tired out.

He was surprised how he liked making houses. He even looked for ways to keep the thing going. But as afternoon fell, he had to admit, like it or not, it was finished. There was nothing more to be done to it.

He was sure no one would find the turtles there and no one ever did. They live there to this day. You can check this for yourself.

CHAPTER 23

THE SUMMER FROLIC

Every Summer there's a day, a particular day, when swamp folk come together for the Frolic. No one knows when it will be. One day it just is and the word goes spreading.

But this year the season was fast passing and still there had been no Frolic. Will decided the time had come.

"Fine day we've been havin," he said to a limpkin-bird, and the limpkin nodded.

"Fact it's an exceptional day," Will went on, and the limpkin nodded again.

"I hear the Frolic's today," Will said, knowing how limpkins are. "You heard anythin about it?"

The limpkin said, "Sir, I cain't say that I have."

And Will said, "Well, that's just what I hear. I might hear wrong. Guess we'd better keep it to ourselves, you and me."

"Oh, of course," the limpkin said, "I unnerstan entirely," and he flew straight off and told everyone he could find.

A limpkin can't keep anything to himself. You hear the limpkins, especially at night, calling out whatever's on their mind, telling any secrets they know. That's how limpkins are.

This Summer Frolic would be on Emma's Island. Everyone but Mr. Took was invited. Panther wouldn't come or Bubba, either, but everyone else would be there. The spiders worked from dawn, weaving web into web, a giant tent among branches, a canopy over half the island. At First Dark, fireflies flew in from every corner. The air was heavy with them, like a starlit sky, descended.

True Dark came and the music of tree frogs spread across the swamp. A chivaree, they called it, a song for everyone.

In a wide clearing, they came. Raccoon, armadillo, bear, possum, owl, egret, heron, turtle, rat, mouse, mole, gator, otter. They talked, played, sang, danced. Some hadn't seen each other since the season before. Old friends met old friends. Enemies weren't sure now why they had parted in anger. They came together, young ones grown older, each quietly checking his progress against the other. *Look, there's Phyllis and Carleton. What they got now? Three boys and a girl? Fine-lookin children, aren't they? Those boys are kind of puny, though, aren't they. And the girl, well, she would look like that, wouldn't she, havin those parents.* They told stories they'd told a hundred times and listened like they had a hundred times. And problems like the drought did not exist.

Celebrations such as this have happened since nobody can remember and they'll happen long after we've been forgotten.

The old alligator came over with Ossie. Will kept to the slough, far off the island, so as not to scare the young ones. Frog-song drifted to him and he was glad to hear it. Ossie found his friends and Emma and they played. All the swamp's children were there and the sound of them was everywhere. It was a fine time, a glad and clamorous time.

Early into that loud night, Ossie heard a sharp "Clavis! Get your butt over here!"

Ossie saw the possum Clavis amble to his father, and for the first time he understood it all.

Clavis's father was thick around the gut, a frown worn into his face. Clavis had two brothers and a sister, the first Ossie knew of them.

The old possum was not happy with a thing in the world. Not a thing was right with it. He was miserable and took it out on his children. He wanted complete attention from them, always. *Yessir, nosir, thankyousir,* they answered him. They were there to do what he told them, and only what he told them. *Yessir, nosir, thankyousir.* They jumped when he barked, the two brothers, the sister. All except Clavis. Clavis didn't jump.

Clavis ignored him. Clavis was playing and singing. His father growled, "Clavis, I won't have you runnin around and singin like a fool!"

The little possum said back, "My name is Lester Whippoorwill and singin is my life."

And to prove it he sang, loud and long.

Clavis's father turned an ugly dark red and shook from anger. The two brothers, the sister, they huddled close to him, scared of him. *Yessir, nosir, thankyousir.* Clavis did not care. Clavis did not care in the least. Clavis sang. His father stomped off, snarling at the other children, "Won't stay here and be humiliated. Come on, we're goin. Let the fool do as he will." *Yessir, nosir, thankyousir.* And they left.

Ossie understood the little possum now. He was no liar. He was a hero.

Ossie and his friends went on playing and the night of the Frolic kept stretching before them. But somehow, slowly, things began to go wrong. There was no moment it happened, no single thing to start it. Still, it did start.

There was a comment here, one there. A heron stepped on a mole's tail. An armadillo insulted a mouse.

And somebody ate a tree snail.

"You just knoooow it was a raccoon," mumbled a squirrel, gossipy.

"I heard what you said," a raccoon said, and sharply.

"I wasn't talkin to you," the squirrel snapped.

"You were talkin *bout* me!"

A kingfisher spoke up. "I didn't hear your name mentioned, friend."

"And I didn't hear anybody ask you," the raccoon said. "And you ain't my friend, friend!"

And on it went and they argued about nothing.

Uncle Will watched from the water and Preacher was with him.

"Lord, it is a spreadin thing," Preacher said. "A foul mood travels twice as fast as Wildfire."

And it was true. Within the course of one more frog-song, everything had fallen apart. The Frolic was coming to a fast unpleasant end. Ossie saw it happening and got the others together and they left. They'd have a good time on their own, somewhere else.

They went off Emma's Island, across a dry prairie. Ossie led. At the far edge of the next hammock, the path dead-ended on a slough. There was a limb, fallen half in water, and they climbed on.

There were twelve of them: Ossie, Emma, Gib, Tudd, Clavis, Stubb, the Quail-Sisters, *the mouse,* and three Rat-Brothers, including the cranky one. "Foot!" They played long into the night, till they were trembling-tired, wrung-out, and had to stop. They fell to heavy sleep, one after the other. They couldn't help it.

Not one of them noticed the limb work loose from the shore. Not one of them knew they were drifting, quietly and surely, away. A silent current pulled them farther and farther from home.

It was hours before the possum Clavis woke up. The world was dark, but he saw it with night-animal eyes. He saw that they weren't where they should be. He woke Tudd the armadillo.

"Aw, good Lord!"

"What is it now?" from Gib.

They all saw. "Aw, good Lord," said Gib.

"GOOD LORD," said Lodemia.

"Good—good—gooooooood Looooooord," said *the mouse*.

"Foot! We're floatin!"

They were, and there was nothing they could do about it. They had no idea how long they'd been floating, how far they'd come, where they were going. Tudd was going over it, to himself, trying to make some sort of plan for them.

"Some of us could swim off this thing," the armadillo was saying, "but what then?" he went on, planning, plotting, "we don't know where we are, so how can we go for help," he wondered, "when we don't know where help is?"

So they drifted.

I have to explain something. This next part of the story was not easy to come by. No one was there to see it happen except those dozen children. After it was over, none of them would talk about it. I'd get pieces of the story, in fits and starts, here and there, but nothing much. I had to put the thing together and make sense of it.

It's based on fact, but I made up some. The conversations are imagined, the rest is invented. An egret gave me descriptions of this distant landscape and I am grateful for that.

They had come to a part of the swamp that was new to them. There was only sawgrass here, moonlit, an open plain that stretched as far as they could see. It was dry, with this one channel running through.

For a long time Ossie stayed watching the watery path behind them. He was sure Uncle Will would come looking for them. Any moment now, he'd see the big old gator swimming in after them. . . .

But the old gator had no idea they were gone. He had no reason to look. So they drifted, farther and farther from home.

"Are you lookin for somethin?" Emma asked him.

"No," Ossie answered, "I'm only lookin."

They drifted and watched the sun rise. They had all grown very quiet. Tudd stared at slow-forming clouds and said nothing. The white owl Gib walked the branch one end to the other and said nothing. They knew something important was happening. They knew their chances of getting back were less and less with each hour, each mile.

"I do not unnerstan, I do not," Gib grumbled to himself, then, louder, "why do we keep movin? The swamp's sittin there. So should we."

They looked and they wondered and Ossie spoke up.

"The swamp doesn't sit," he said. "It's a river, always movin."

". . . Is that true?" asked Clavis, the possum who had never cared about the truth of *anything*.

Tudd the armadillo shrugged.

Gib didn't care. "Awright, it's a river. Where's it takin us?"

Nobody had an answer.

Lodemia watched the water. "IT HAS TO STOP SOME-WHERE."

Tudd scratched an ear. "Does it?"

Ossie climbed higher on a branch and could see nothing but more swamp.

"Maybe it doesn't," Emma said.

"Look, here's the deal," Gib said. He was close to crying.

"All I want is to go home," he said. And then he did cry. He cried softly at first, then with sobs, and finally everything pouring out. He lost all control of it, hacking, bawling, wailing, trembling.

None of the others had ever seen the little white owl like this. He had never been like this. Gib, their sort of leader, the one who kept games going. *Look, here's the deal,* he'd say and he'd handle it. Gib, who outsmarted the King Snake. But this was too much, this he could not handle.

The others looked away.

Ossie thought he could answer Gib's question. He thought he knew where the river was taking them. It was taking them to the mangroves. But he did not tell the others that. Gib cried himself out and sat there, exhausted, and nobody said a word except,

"Foot."

In the hours that came next, they were mostly quiet. Ossie and Emma sat together, on a higher limb, and watched the swamp drift past them. They talked once in a while, but mostly just kept to their thoughts.

Now Ossie, like many swamp folk, had a corner of his brain, off to the side and toward the back, that he kept for himself. He made a dream-world there and he'd go to it now and then and add a thing or two. Sometimes he'd get rid of a thing or two. In the last days and weeks, it was all about Emma there. He'd imagine conversations between them and he'd call her Emmadear, dear Emma, dear Emma dear. He thought up a whole future for them there, a rat-lodge, two children, a boy and a girl.

Then Emma said suddenly, "Oh, Ossie! I remember! We *did* see butterflies."

"We sure did, Emmadear," he heard himself say.

And he went still. Dead still. Had he done that? Did he call her Emmadear and right to her face? Was he *sure* he said Emmadear?

Yeah, he was sure. Emmadear. He said it. He saw it in her face. There was nothing to do about it. He stared at her as she stared at him. He smiled, all he could think to do.

She said, "Did you call me dear?"

There was no point lying, so he said, "Yeah, I guess."

She said, "I thought so." And then she said nothing for a short while.

It was the longest short while of Ossie's life.

Then Emma laughed and said, "Allright, Ossiedear," and kissed him. Just a quick brush of a kiss, but that's what it was. It was a kiss.

The swamp changed around them now in quiet and simple ways. There were fewer tree islands, farther between. There was no shade and the sun hit hard and made them sleepy. And still on they went.

CHAPTER 24

BACK IN A LAND OF WOOD SAGE

They were asleep when the branch came to rest on an island.

Here in the middle of a swamp, flat and hot, here was a place of beautiful green. It was tall and thick and a cool breeze came from it.

There was something about it, something familiar to Ossie, but he didn't know what. He moved onto land. Under the trees, shadows washed away the sting of the heat. The air was weighted with orchid-smell. The others followed Ossie in, toward the center of it, to a deep round pool ringed by tall cypress.

Now he saw why he knew this place. "There are berries, over there, past the ferns," he said.

It was Will's Island. Ossie hadn't seen it in a long time, but nothing was changed. It seemed untouched by the drought, everything as alive and full and green as ever. Uncle Will had told him it would be like this. The pond was deep and feeding the island. And no one else was there. It was a secret still.

Ossie went looking for a tree he remembered. It was taller than the rest, too tall for the others to climb. Maybe he could see their own island from it.

They waited as he climbed. When he reached the high branches, he was gone from their view. But still they watched.

He was at the top, where limbs grew thin, far above other trees. Hot wind blew from the grassy swamp and the world stretched, endless, in every possible direction. Now and again, islands rose in the distance, dark brown spots on a wide brown prairie. Over it all, clouds towered, overpowered. And he could see everything but what he was looking for.

They weren't surprised when he told them. Not one of them expected to see home or family again. Gib bobbed, not talking. Emma seemed allright, but quiet. Tudd scratched the ground. Lodemia cried, quietly, and Philomena went to her. Stubb either accepted it or didn't understand it. Who could tell with Stubb? *the mouse* looked worried, but *the mouse* always looked worried. Clavis yawned and fell asleep. Ossie felt bad for them all.

It was Tudd who said it first. He said the island would make a good place to live. It had everything they needed, it was nicer than what they'd left behind.

And it *was* a good place. Uncle Will's Gator Hole was deep with fresh water, from somewhere far within. The bushes were full with berries, the ground with worms and bugs. There were plenty of places to nest or burrow. The trees were strong and would protect them from storms. The more they saw, the more they liked.

They could live here and be happy, they knew that. It would not be like it was back *there*, where the drought had turned everyone selfish and angry.

And so the first day passed into night.

They spent their days foraging food or off on some game. Nights usually found them gathering and talking until they were ready for sleep. They talked about things they'd found or seen or how they'd done this or done that. Some nights they told stories. One night Emma told a tale she'd heard from the manatee, Rufus. And it was this.

The Tale of the Great Flood

The swamp was once full of folk and they got along good. Nobody took anythin more than they needed to get by. And what they took, they thanked the Master of Breath for it.

Things went this way for ages and all was good.

But then, over a long slow time, things started changin. Folk got forgetful. They forgot about not takin too much, and sayin thanks and such.

The Master of Breath warned em once and then twice. "Take only what y'all need," He said, "and share what there is." And they'd remember, a day or two. Then they'd forget.

They treated the swamp awful poor.

Finally, the Master of Breath got fed up. He figured He'd teach em a real lesson. So He made a drought across the swamp and the riches of the earth dried up and blew away as dust.

"Where'd everythin go?" folk asked. "We need us a good rain!"

The Master of Breath said, "Forget it. This is all there is now." He sent an Unspoken Word through the swamp, tellin everybody to stop and gather together. *Share* was the Word, *take what's left and use it careful.*

But they ignored the Unspoken Word and they acted worse than before. They got greedier. They fought over whatever was left. Soon, they were murderin each other over single drops of water. This was a terrible time. A awful, awful time.

The Master of Breath told the swamp folk, "I'm givin y'all one last chance. And I mean it. You folk *got* to straighten up!"

And again they did not listen. "Nothin wrong here," they said, "that a good rain wouldn't fix."

Then the Master of Breath lost His temper. "You want rain," He said, "I'll give you rain!"

And He sent onto those folk the worst storm ever, as bad as a dozen hurricanes piled one on top of the other! Folk ran to the forests and huddled among the shelterin trees. But the Master sent winds to find em. And the winds ripped trees from the ground and the rain beat down on the swamp and drove those folk to their knees.

And the Master of Breath felt no pity for em.

He lifted the ocean out of the sea and drove it across the land. A wave, higher than the tallest cypress, rolled over the face of the swamp.

Most of em were swept off with it, and never seen again. The few that lived were screamin and beggin for mercy.

Finally, the Master called off the storm. The flood drained and the land appeared again, a ruin now. Only a handful of folk were left livin, no more than two of each kind.

The Master of Breath gave em one last and final warnin. "Y'all cain't forget this lesson," He said, "or if you do, I'll send another storm down and it'll be a baaaaaaad one! So y'all better get along and start treatin this place with some re-spect," He said.

The folk that were left sort of nodded, not sayin a word.

And the Master of Breath said, "Y'all got to remember, the swamp is a River of water and the river of Water is Life."

And the swamp folk said they'd remember. And to this day, when drought comes, they hear the Unspoken Word. And strife is forgotten and folk gather together and share what little there is.

Ossie wondered now about the tale. He thought about the

folk at the Frolic. If there really *was* an Unspoken Word, wasn't this the time for it to be heard?

Within a few days more, the little ones were used to this place. They had built themselves burrows and nests and lodges. They thought less about where they'd come from and they grew used to where they were. This was home. It was good.

CHAPTER 25
AGAIN

It might have gone on forever that way, but it didn't. It ended in the middle of a long afternoon.

They were hiding, seeking, when they heard the little quail Lodemia call out, a yell, a scared scream. Ossie raced to find her and, one after the other, they jumped from their hiding places: Emma in a patch of a wild petunia, Gib the owl burrowed among some roots, the armadillo Tudd under an old log, and Stubb the turtle . . . Well, Stubb was somewhere. Together they ran across the island, full-speed.

They ran right into Lodemia, crying for them to RUN-RUNRUN! Then they saw the snake, Mr. Took, coming at them with his ungainly grace. So this was where the old beast had been hiding. The little ones stopped, stuck where they were with fear.

THE TALE OF THE SWAMP RAT

"Fooooooooot!" was what the grumpy rat said.

The snake was worse than Ossie remembered—bigger, thicker, nastier, his face even more battered. Now he truly looked like the monster he was.

They turned. They ran. And the snake went after them.

Ahead was a giant mahogany tree, fallen to block the path. One by one they made their way up it. When Lodemia slipped, Clavis and Tudd hurried to help. They were all on the top of it, ready to jump, when the old wood gave way under them. The tree was only a shell, its insides rotted away. Branches big and small were crumbling, collapsing, and the group of them fell to the ground on the other side.

They seemed allright at first. A little dazed and surprised, but allright.

But a heavy limb had fallen on Emma's leg and she was trapped. They went to work on the branch, fast as they could, and soon she pulled herself free. Her leg wasn't broken, but swelling already, and she couldn't walk fast.

The snake was still coming, only the wrecked log between them. Emma would not be able to outrun Mr. Took. She knew this and was scared. They were all scared.

"Go on," Ossie said to her, "go ahead and get goin." But she didn't, she waited. "Go however fast you can, get however far you can!"

Tudd nudged her on. "We'll slow him down."

She nodded and ran as best she could. Ossie and the others saw her disappear, then they ran down a different path to confuse the snake. They hurried across a weedy field and stopped. Ossie listened and heard Mr. Took coming.

"Let me see what I can do," came a voice. It was Stubb, and no one had seen him get there. "Reckon I should be able to help."

Ossie wasn't sure what good Stubb could do, but the snake was half the way across the field and the little turtle was already heading toward him. The swamp rat waited and watched and saw the snake attack. Stubb was closed tight in his shell as Mr. Took struck at him again and again. Ossie didn't want to think what it was like, inside that shell.

The rest of them were running and Ossie caught up to them. "He'll be comin after us soon. He'll know Stubb is stallin him."

"Then what?" Gib asked. "Then what'll we do?" He was bobbing, up, down, wild, panicky.

"We'll be allright," Tudd told him, slow, easy.

"But how, how, how! We'll never get away from him," the little owl cried.

"Right now he's trackin us," the armadillo explained, "but I got a plan to throw him *off* our track." Ossie saw how Tudd was calming Gib, so carefully no one knew he was doing it. "You can help us, can't you, Gib?" Tudd started explaining his plan, making it up as he went along.

The Quail-Sisters could move faster than the snake, Tudd knew that. He put them on a side path and told them, "When he comes, you act like you don't see him. Philomena, play you're worried about your sister. Lodemia, you'll be bawlin and wailin."

"NO PROBLEM," Lodemia said.

And Tudd went on, "When he's close, go runnin that way. Till you get to Gib."

• • •

Then Tudd gave Gib his part to play. One by one, he set them all in place, even *the mouse*.

Mr. Took was giving up on Stubb about now and heading off to find the others. The turtle was still in his shell and safe—though he'd gotten dizzy enough to throw up and it was in there with him, not smelling too good.

The snake found the young quail Lodemia crying, Philomena at her side, and he fell for their act all the way. He moved in on them, careful, without a sound. He was just about there, closer and closer still. He could almost taste them. His gut was knotting, hungry. He was coiling, rising, and . . .

The Quail-Sisters went running, his lunch went running away from him. Mr. Took said a thing I won't repeat here and went after them.

Lodemia and Philomena led him down a twisting path, farther from Emma. They led him in a big slow circle, tiring him out, just as the armadillo had told them. In another moment, Gib jumped in and led the snake.

Tudd watched from a tree limb, proud to see how well it was working.

As he brought Mr. Took by Clavis, Gib called at a whisper, "Your turn," to the possum.

But Clavis had fallen asleep. Mr. Took came still closer and still Clavis slept.

Gib ran to Tudd, bobbing, bobbing. "He's sleepin! What do I do, what do I do?!"

Tudd only told him to *shhh!*, and they watched.

Mr. Took was right on Clavis, near striking distance. The possum was snoring. Mr. Took relaxed. This one would be easy.

Then Clavis was gone, just like that, and the snake barely saw him shoot away. Clavis was up a cabbage palm, scooting high up its knobby trunk.

Tudd said to Gib, "Nobody plays possum like a possum plays possum."

Clavis crawled higher in the palm, jumped to the branches of a pond apple tree, and off through even more trees. Mr. Took said another bad thing and hissed and cursed and sputtered and spat, too angry to control himself.

The rest of them met Emma and Ossie near the hammock shore. They had slowed the snake, tired him, left him immobilized by his own fury. But they hadn't stopped him. He'd get it together, he'd be back.

They knew this.

But they didn't know what to do next. They could head north, into a wide prairie, but there would be no places to hide. And Emma could only move slowly.

Still, there wasn't much choice. They had to get off that island.

They turned to go and it was too late. He was there. Mr. Took blocked their one path. He smiled a crooked smile and said, "Y'all're just children, ain't you? Y'all're still learnin tricks to fool poor Mr. Took, don't you see? But don't you think I know those tricks by now? Don't I know *all* the tricks? So ain't we wastin time, y'all's and mine?"

Then he saw Ossie and his crooked smile grew even bigger.

"Ohhhhh, who is this here? Is it who I think it is? It is, isn't it?" The snake's voice was as beat-up as his face.

Ossie told his friends to run and they did. Mr. Took didn't mind. Mr. Took only cared about the swamp rat.

"Yeah, you and me know each other, don't we?"

Ossie saw, off to his side, a wall of heavy-grown vines. If he could get to them, the snake would have trouble following.

"We're like fambly, aren't we?"

Mr. Took had a coward's heart. Like any good coward, he believed in nothing. Absolutely nothing. Not even his own words. Everything he said, he asked, a question.

But of course his bite was full of poison and that had to count for something. When he struck, Ossie would tremble as the snake's venom moved through him. There would be a quick feverish burning. His legs would fold under him, useless. He would grow blind. His chest would strangle, breath coming harder and then not at all. That's what Mr. Took could do. That counted for something.

"Remember when I saw you last?" Ossie watched how the snake slid closer each time he spoke. "You were with your own sweet fambly, weren't you? And they were sweet, all of em, weren't they?" He was already near enough to strike.

The snake was rising and Ossie knew the time to go was now. And he went. The snake struck fast, so fast he might have disappeared from the earth for a time. But Ossie wasn't there when he hit. Ossie had started running, one exact moment before.

Mr. Took struck hard into the ground. He wasn't happy, but another bruise on that face wouldn't much matter.

Ossie ran into the vines, faster and faster, even as they grew thick around him. Mr. Took went tearing in, stalks snapping, splintering. Confused shadows cut everywhere.

But Ossie was gone. He was nowhere. And there were everywhere vines. It made the snake mad and made him push deeper. Here, it grew dark and vines didn't break under him.

Mr. Took felt the stalks squeezing. He was getting stuck. He caught quick sight of the swamp rat racing ahead, through shadows, but there was no way to get to him. The snake was thrashing and screaming out in his rage. Mr. Took had never been as angry as this and it wasn't pretty to see.

Ossie went for the others and found them by the water, on the big tree branch that had brought them. There was nowhere farther to go. It was a matter of time, and not much, before Mr. Took would get there. They were screaming at Ossie, "What do we do?" "Where do we go?" "How do we get away from that thing?" "Foot!"

Then *the mouse* spoke up. "If you don't mind my sayin, I don't think we can expect Ossie to have all the—the—the answers for us. I think we—we—we are in this together."

And then the owl Gib whipped around and said, "Yeah, but I don't really care what you think. Ossie's the one who got us here in the first place."

"Oh, well, I—I—I unnerstan what you're sayin of course. But what I mean to say is—"

"Is what?" Gib yelled. "What is it you mean to say! Why don't you just come out and say it!" And he turned to the others. "I'm sick of listenin to *the mouse* stammerin and stutterin!"

the mouse had had enough. "And who cares what you think . . . you—you—YOU DUMB FOOL!" He screamed that last part. It was the loudest, angriest thing he had ever said.

Clavis, like everybody, was impressed. "Whooooa. Who'd've thought *the mouse* had it in him."

"And my name is not *the mouse*! My parents did NOT say, let's call him *the mouse*! I—HAVE—A—NAME—YOU—KNOW!"

But the whole thing had taken so much out of him, he never got around to telling them what it was. With all the yelling, they didn't notice the old branch moving, floating free. Emma felt it first and said, "Y'all." They looked at her.

She said, "We're floatin," simply.

They were. Ossie ran to the end of the branch and looked in the water.

Uncle Will was pushing them along with his snout. "Time you children were gettin home," he said.

As they drifted, they said little. They only wanted to be back, to be home, to be with family. They wanted things to be as they had been.

But Ossie wasn't sure. He wasn't sure that could happen, not after what they'd been through. They weren't as young as they had been and never would be again. They moved against the slow current and no one noticed that Summer was turning into Fall.

PART THREE

A HARDSHELL WORLD

CHAPTER 26

THE TRUTH AND WHAT IT'S WORTH

A Fish only swims in so much water.
—a swamp saying

The swamp folk thought they'd never see the children again. But here they were, on a fine Fall day, and no worse than when they left. Maybe better. Except Emma and her leg, but that would heal. Everyone was glad and laughing, until the Prophet Bubba yelled for them to "Stop! Listen to me!"

He said to them, "Don't act like a buncha fools, you buncha fools! These ain't your children! These are ghosts of em, returned from the dead! Their spirits have escaped the mangroves! They're here to haunt us all!"

The swamp folk grew quiet. They backed off from the young ones. They were afraid.

"Bubba," said a skunk, that old and crotchety one, "looks to me like Uncle Will brung em home." The big gator lolled in the water and nodded to them.

"Oh. I see," mumbled the Prophet. "So it is. Well. This changes things. This is somethin altogether other."

The swamp folk ran out to see Will and thank him and Bubba could only watch.

Yes, yes, yes, the Prophet said, of course the old gator can do great things. Will has snatched these poor children from the Grasp of Death. He is a Grand Soul, the old gator. Let us Sing his Praises.

With or without Bubba, this was a good time. The children were home and everyone was happy for it. (But even then, Ossie began to hear their whispers. And their whispers were about him. *I never noticed that child before, did you? Where'd he come from anyway? Just who is he anyhow?* He tried not to hear, but he heard.)

The Prophet Bubba heard the whispers, too, and it was just what he wanted to hear. Soon as he heard, he knew what he had to do. He didn't waste a minute but got right at it.

The thing about Bubba was this: Bubba looked at the world in Bubba-terms. The way he saw it, the world was full of opportunities to make his-own-self better off than he was. *Any* opportunity, way he saw it, was worth taking. And Ossie was nothing if not opportunity.

The Prophet took folk aside, one by one.

He told them there were signs. "Lookit how deep the water draws into the earth. Now we can walk to most ever island! There are no boundaries holdin us back. This is one of the signs. This means somethin Evil has come amongst us." They should know this without his telling them.

"A curse has been put upon us," he told them, "by this Evil thing."

Who, they wanted to know, who was this Evil thing? Was it the gopher turtles?

"No! Listen to me!" said, yelled the Prophet Bubba. "It is the little swamp rat who's bringin this curse!"

Gib's father knew the Prophet was right. "I always thought so but din't want to say it aloud."

Some looked for reasons not to believe, but Bubba made sure they did. He told them a thing they had not known, till now.

"Listen to me! You've heard of the One the Snake Spared, haven't you!"

Yes, I know the story, don't you? I heard about the rat-fambly, didn't you? Ten babies, wasn't it? Twelve, and the parents. Mr. Took got them. Got them all. All but that one. The One Who Was Spared.

"Well, this is him! This stranger! The swamp rat is the One Who Was Spared!"

They hadn't known this, not till now.

"Mr. Took never spares, does he!" Bubba said, yelled. "Never! Less he is *afraid* of the swamp rat! Less the swamp rat is far more powerful than Mr. Took!"

Now it all made sense. Now the swamp folk worried. The Prophet Bubba was always right and about everything.

"Look at him," Bubba told them, "look and see how he is marked. This is a sign that cannot be ignored."

The next time, they looked. And they saw the scar. And no one doubted the Prophet.

• • •

It wasn't long until Will heard these things. He found Preacher and asked him to go to the Ironhead Stork. Maybe the old heron could talk sense into him. "S'pose I could try," said Preacher. "Can't guarantee anythin. But s'pose I can try," said Preacher, who liked being needed far more than he ever let on.

Preacher found the Prophet Bubba in a thick oak, very much asleep, the ground below a lacework of old fish parts. As Preacher flew in, he could hear the stork's snores.

"Lo, Bubba?" Preacher said. But Bubba slept. The heron flew to a branch right over him. "Yoo-hoo!" Bubba was sleeping a just sleep. Preacher *ahem*ed a few times and flapped out his wings. "Hey, ya big lazy prophet!" he yelled. Bubba half-started waking. He belched once and fish-smell filled the air.

"Mornin, Bubba."

". . . Howdy, Preacher."

The heron gave him another while to wake up, then he said, "Fine day," with a wide smile.

"Fine it is," the Prophet Bubba said, yawned.

"Fact it's an exceptional day we've been havin."

Bubba nodded and rubbed at his eyes.

"Like as not, the rest of it should be, too," Preacher went on and Bubba was pretty much awake now. "So what's this mess of lies you been spreadin bout the swamp rat!"

"Whaaaaaaaaaaaaaaaaaaat!?" the Prophet Bubba nearly fell off the branch.

Preacher tore in on him. "You know there's nothin wrong with that child!"

"Oh, but, I—!"

Preacher didn't let up. "He's got nobody to stand up for him, that's the only reason you're goin after him!"

"Now, that's not the case, I—!"

"You're scarin folk with this talk of curses and what-all!"

"Listen to me, Preacher, I—!"

"Bubba, I've known you since you were fresh outta the egg and I know you don't believe in signs and omens and what-all!"

"Where'd you hear that!?" shouted the Prophet Bubba, very awake.

"Come on, bird to bird. You don't believe that junk any more than I do!"

The Ironhead Stork flew close to Preacher, riled. "Now hold on, Preacher! I, unlike you, have a gift to find meanin where there ain't none! I, unlike you, can unnerstan that which makes no sense!"

"Aw, Bubba," groaned Preacher.

"Let me ask you a thing, Preach. Are the swamp folk a buncha idiots?"

"Course not."

"Have they chose to believe what I tell em?"

"Some of em have, Bubba."

"Does your friend the swamp rat have a mark upon him?"

"It's a scar, you old toot."

"And a scar is a mark and I have explained its meanin to these folk who are not idiots!"

Preacher ran that back through his brain. Bubba's thoughts could be as hard to follow as his own.

"The swamp folk think I'm right," the Prophet Bubba said, almost shouting, "so I must be right!"

Preacher shook his head, disbelieving what he was hearing. "Bubba, it's one thing to lie. It's an altogether other thing to fall for it yourself."

At that, the Prophet Bubba flew wildly off into the forest, fast disappearing among the trees. From somewhere out there, his voice came screaming back, "It's only a lie when nobody believes it!"

Preacher went to the others, one by one, and talked to them about Ossie. He told them how he'd come to know the boy and the time they'd spent with Uncle Will, on those long Summer days. It was true, the boy had an unusual start on life. But this nonsense about curses was no more than that, nonsense!

By the end of that day, Preacher had gotten to most of them. It seemed they believed him, most of them. He hoped they believed him. But he wasn't as sure as he wanted to be.

CHAPTER 27

AN ELEPHANT DREAM

It was solid into Fall now and all chance for rain was gone. Ossie found Will that morning and the gator was deep in a sleep. "Uncle Will." He said it, a whisper. "You allright?"

The gator opened his eyes but didn't say anything.

Ossie thought the better of it and left. Will was off in a dream.

Later, he told Ossie a third Dream. And here it is.

There were other Worlds before this. The land's changed many times, many ways. Us gators have been around since the Start and we seen it all.

We saw the Swamp when the Elephant walked. A father of my father saw and remembered and now I remember, too. I remember the Elephant they called Mammoth.

He was big, as tall at the shoulder as I am long. He was

covered in fur, brown and thick, with tusks long and curvin, and the Swamp shook when he walked it.

The Gator saw him come, the Gator heard him come. The Elephant came from the other side of this World and the land was dry where Oceans are now. Brother Mammoth and his family walked the dry land and as they walked the Water rose behind them. A new Ocean lapped their heels and covered their footsteps and still they walked.

The Gator saw em come, Elephants marchin across time in an endless line. They made families and raised children and the Swamp was their home. Other folk came, too. There was a Tiger, twice as big as Panther. There were Dragonflies the size of Hawk.

And these were the creatures of the Swamp. For more years than can be counted, the Swamp was their Home.

But the years became Centuries and those passed in thousands. The land grew Warm. The World didn't suit Brother Mammoth anymore. He left the Swamp and he left the World. Brother Tiger went with him. But the land stayed and the Swamp stayed.

And the Gator stayed.

There were different Worlds before this. There will be different Worlds after. Not a thing endures but what's in an Alligator's Dream.

An itchy dry wind rolled over the grassy plain, a stale and crackling wind full of dust from a dead dry land. The face of the swamp had changed and everyone in it was changing, too.

That next day, Ossie went to see his friends and they were not there. He thought they were only late, so he waited. He waited until morning was midday and no one came. His shadow stretched below him and he went looking for them.

• • •

The possum Clavis was with his father, two brothers, and a sister. They were in a tree, asleep, all but Clavis. He was staring off, just staring off.

"Clavis!" Ossie called up, quiet. Now the possum played he was asleep and Ossie called again. "Clavissss!"

"Yeah, what's the problem?" Clavis snapped, still pretending to sleep.

"That's what I'm wonderin."

"What's what you're wonderin?"

"What the problem is, Clavis."

"There's no problem I know of," the possum grunted, angry.

"Then what're you doin?" Ossie asked, still whispered.

"What's it look like? I'm sleepin," Clavis said, eyes shut to prove it.

"How can you tell me you're sleepin if you're sleepin?" Ossie asked.

"Maybe I talk in my sleep."

Ossie wanted to know why his friend was in this foul mood. "Why won't you tell me what's the matter? Where is everybody?"

"Not here," the possum mumbled, grumbled. "Now go away, let me sleep." And he closed his eyes and went to sleep.

Ossie climbed partway up the tree, careful not to wake the rest of the family. "I will if you tell me what's up," he said. "Why aren't you playin?"

"I'm sick," Clavis said. "Allright?"

"Oh," Ossie said. "Allright. Sorry."

"Hold on," said Clavis. "I'm lyin." He checked that the

others were still sleeping, then he crawled closer to the swamp rat and told him, "It's like this, Ossie. My father doesn't want me runnin around all day. You know?"

"Since when do you care what your father wants?"

"I don't," Clavis answered, and quick, "but he has part of a point. I'm nocturnal. I'm s'posed to be awake at night. You can't be nocturnal in the middle of broad daylight. You know?"

Ossie nodded. "Yeah, I guess." And he started down the tree. "Maybe I'll see you later then."

And Clavis said, "Yeah. Right. Later." And then he said, "Hold on. I'm lyin again. Not later. Never. You know?"

Ossie didn't know. But the possum was climbing back to his family. So the swamp rat left.

When he came onto Tudd with his family, the armadillo said, "Aw, good Lord, Ossie."

"You want to play?"

Tudd shook his head. "Can't. Mom and Dad think I'm too old for it. They want me actin my age. That's what they say, but—"

"Tudd?" his father called. "Where you at, boy? You need to be back over here with your family, allrighty?"

The armadillo only mumbled, "Sorry," and went. And Ossie heard him saying, over and over, "Good Lord, good Lord, good Lord."

It was the same wherever he went. "Look, here's the deal," Gib told him. "My folks say I'm a growin boy and a growin boy needs his rest. They say that."

When he saw the Rat-Brothers, one of them yelled, "Foot!"

and they ran off into the woods. Ossie did not understand what was happening.

But when he found Emma, she told him the truth. "We're not s'posed to talk to you. We're not s'posed to talk *about* you."

"No kiddin," Ossie said. "Any special reason?"

She shrugged. All the parents, she said, blamed him for the children floating off and getting lost. The Prophet had gotten to them. Ossie, the Prophet was saying, had brought some sort of curse on the swamp.

"You got a reputation, Ossie. It's pretty bad."

He said, "Oh."

And then Johnny saw them. "Daaaaaaad! He's here! It's him!"

And Emma said, "You better go."

Ossie was going to say more, but Emma hurried into the lodge. And he went.

CHAPTER 28

INTO THE DEVIL'S GARDEN

He went and did not stop. He ran all that day, through the night, into the next morning. He didn't stop until the sun was setting on another day. By now he had run through Big Cypress, into a pine forest. Here the trees grew tall and straight and the ground was hard. Scrub palmettos were everywhere. He was lost, again, and this time he wanted to be.

He was running when he ran right into something. It was the head of a deer, a big doe, grazing. The doe screeched and rared onto hind legs and tried to kill Ossie. Her hooves tore at the dry ground and the swamp rat darted, here, there, anywhere to get away. The doe was wild with anger, snuffing and snorting and trying to trample Ossie.

"Leave me alone, you little . . . !" she was yelling. "I'll kill

you, you little . . . ! Little . . . ! You . . . ! You . . . little . . ."
Then she saw. "You're nothin but a swamp rat."

Ossie got up from the dust and said, "Yeah. That's what I
am."

The doe did not grow calm, but only more furious. "Just
how STOOOOPID are you!? Tell me how STOOPID are
you!?"

"I'm not sure," Ossie told her, "but I think I'm pretty
stupid."

"Why'd you sneak up on me like that!? I thought you were
a hunter!"

Ossie couldn't see how she'd think that, but he didn't say
anything.

"They could be anywhere, the hunters, any place, any
time," the doe was yelling, eyes cutting this way, that. "You
can't let your guard down! Can't relax! That's the way it is in
these woods!"

It didn't seem much of a life to Ossie, but again he didn't
say anything.

"I go it alone," she was saying, "easier that way. I'm ready
to run in a second. Nobody to worry bout but me." She
looked around Ossie, searching. "Where are the others?"

"Other whats?"

"Swamp rats. You folk always move in groups."

"Not always," Ossie told her.

Her eyes lit up. "No kiddin? It's just you?"

He nodded. Just him.

"Ha!" she said. "Knew it! You're not so stoopid as you
look! Knew it!"

He said, "Thank you."

"Where you goin, swamp rat?"

"Don't know." And he shrugged.

"Ha!" she said. "Knew it! You don't make plans. You're ready for anythin."

Ossie half-nodded back.

"Where'd you come from?" she asked.

"Hard to say."

"No family?"

"No," he told her.

"No friends?"

He shook his head.

"Ha!" she said. "Knew it! *You*, little fellow, are practically intelligent!"

He thanked her again and suddenly she said, "What was that?!"

"What was what?"

"That! Did you hear?"

Ossie heard nothing and said so.

She said to him, quickly, quietly, "Look, little fellow. You don't need me. You got nothin to hold you down, you come from nowhere, leavin nobody. You'll do great!" And suddenly she was darting off into the woods. "You'll find your own way!"

And she was gone. Like that. She left him there with those words. *Find your own way.* Did he have anywhere to find his way to?

Ossie set off again, deeper into the pines and beyond and day became night and he was in the Devil's Garden. He stopped to rest.

And that's when he noticed that something was making him nervous. The feeling had sneaked up on him, overtaking him. But what made him this way? He smelled at the air. He smelled nothing. No snake, no Mr. Took. He listened. He heard a breeze move through the trees over him.

Or was it a breeze? He looked to the branches, but there was only darkness. He heard it again. And he saw a shadow move slowly in the trees. He took a step away. The shadow stepped, too. When he moved faster, the shadow moved faster. Wherever he went, the shadow went. He stopped and it stopped.

He heard a low rumbled breath and he knew. It was Panther. In another moment, and only for a moment, he saw eyes shine over him.

Ossie was trembling. He couldn't just stand here. He had to run, had to try, so he took a breath and jumped, running, into the scrub. He didn't look back.

But Panther was with him, above him, moving easily in the branches. When there were no trees, Panther followed on the ground. Ossie saw a shallow creek ahead in the moonlight and splashed through. Panther took it in one leap.

The path narrowed. Ossie darted into palmettos. Still Panther was there. A trail widened to a clearing and Ossie had to cross it.

But then Panther was in front of him, waiting.

Ossie stopped, each breath burning holes in his throat. Panther's own breath was slow and calm. There came a voice, and it was hard and rugged for a cat.

"What you think you're doin here?"

Ossie tried to answer, "I don't think I know wha—"

But Panther was talking over him. "This ain't no place for a swamp rat."

"No, it isn't, is it?"

"Don't smartmouth me," Panther said, almost growled.

And Ossie kept quiet.

Panther circled him, slow, and said, "You got good reason for bein here?"

Ossie shook his head, no.

"You got *any* reason?"

Again he shook his head, no.

"Then get out. Ain't no place for a swamp rat. Go back where you were and go now."

With that, Panther was gone. Ossie waited, too scared to move. He listened to what few sounds there were, what few sounds he could hear over the beat of his heart. Then he turned and started back to where he'd been.

He found the way home without much trouble.

CHAPTER 29
BURNING RIVER

Nobody saw it start. There had been heat lightning in the swamp. That must have got it going. Tudd was first to see a wispy fog in the distance, a ragged cloud. Soon they *all* knew it was fire.

Fire, as the swamp folk see it, is a living thing. It crosses the swamp with reason and thought. There's only one fire, they believe. All fire is the same fire, always moving. It comes to clean when the swamp has grown thick and new life is choked out. It is slow moving and lets folk get out of the way. It leaves when it's finished and goes some other where.

But every now and then, fire gets in a mood.

It turns mean and crazy and spiteful and they call it Wildfire. Uncle Will said that rain can chase Wildfire, but can't kill it. Wildfire changes shape and size and hides from rain. It can even hide under the ground, still burning.

Swamp folk know that fire will always be with them. Sometimes it leaves, sometimes for long stretches. But they know it will come back. And now it was here.

One by one, they gathered. The fire was still far off, no reason for fear just yet. It was something to sit and watch.

Preacher flew out for a look and returned with the news.

"It's wild, allright. Nothin but dry grass between here and there," Preacher said, circling big and slow overhead. "It's hop, skip, and jumpin all across the prairie. Got a ornery streak in it. Worse than Big Joe. Goin to be what-all to deal with."

The fire was only now crawling over the horizon. All through the morning they watched.

By afternoon, they knew Preacher was right. The fire grew fatter, smoke boiling and roiling into the clouds. It was *very* wild. Uncle Will figured it would be here in a day. By morning, they'd start moving.

When night came, the fire's yellowed glow lit the swamp. Folk watched and watched until they were too tired to watch. Ossie stayed longer. The fire had no smell and no sound, and the little rat did not know it would change his world forever.

The next day had a hard time coming. The sun rose under heavy gray smoke. Ossie and the others woke to the first scent of the fire. A green snake came from the prairie, hurrying through. "I seen fire in my time," said the snake, "but this one's in a awful hissy mood! There's only one thing to do, and that's get out of the way!"

Will knew it would take powerful rain to stop the Wildfire.

A good five-day flooder could fill the swamp, chase the fire to high land, and trap it.

But there was no rain coming. This fire would have its way with them.

Now for Prophet, the fire was only another of those opportunities he loved so much. He sure wasn't going to let this one slip by.

"Listen to me!" he said to the swamp folk. "I have tried to warn you, but you will not listen to me! When will you LISTEN!?!" he screamed. "Why is this Wildfire here!? I ask you, WHY?!"

But no one could tell him why.

"I'll tell you," he went on. "It's cause of that little swamp rat!"

Ossie wasn't there. He was with Preacher, watching the Wildfire.

"Listen to me!" the Prophet shouted, "We must—"

And then there was a rumble like thunder. It was Uncle Will. "Folk," he said, very deep, very low. Everyone turned from Prophet, like he'd disappeared into thin air. "I think there's somethin else we ought listen to," Will went on.

They listened, or tried, but couldn't hear. You may remember, there's a thing in the swamp they call Unspoken Word and you hear it once in a while. No one speaks, but it spreads all at once.

Will heard. The word was *Go*.

The alligator said, "It's time." He said, "We best start movin."

And they did.

"No, n-n-no, no, no," the Prophet was stuttering, sputtering. "Listen to me—listen—we stay here and—and we—and—!"

Will did not pause to look back. He went and the swamp folk went with him.

The ancient gator set across the dry prairie, headed west, and they followed. They followed Will and forgot the Prophet Bubba. Rabbit, possum, mole, armadillo, raccoon, frog, snail, turtle, heron, egret, snake, rat, mouse, all of them, all of them left with Will.

The Prophet was so angry, spit dribbled from his beak. Then he saw the fire crawling closer and he left, too, headed off on his own.

Ossie didn't go, not at first. He was looking for Emma. He saw her family cross a waterless pond, but she wasn't with them. He called to one of her brothers, to a sister—"Where's Emma? Have you seen her?"—but no one would answer him. He tried to get to them, but he was pushed away by an endless animal stream going the other way.

He shot up a tree and still could not see Emma. He was afraid she'd been left behind in the mad rushing. He went to find her.

It wasn't easy moving against this great moving crowd.

"The fool's goin the wrong way!" "Who cares, let him go!"

As more of them left, things thinned out. Ossie ran quickly into the swamp forest.

When he got to Emma's home, it was empty. "Emma!" He ran everywhere, calling for her. He checked the vines; maybe she'd gotten caught. "Emmaaaaaa!" He checked every rat-lodge he could find; maybe she'd been hurt. He looked and found nothing. The fire was closer, its smell was rotten and sour. But he kept looking and calling, *"Emmaaaaaaaaaaaa!"*

He was in a tree when it happened. A hot wind blew in, folding every leaf, and Ossie saw. The fire was there, wrapped in gray smoke, the smoke alive with embers and whole burning branches.

Wildfire found its voice, a terrible cracking, spitting, roaring. It was the sound of dry grass falling to flame, it was the sap of trees boiling and exploding, it was the sound of the end of everything.

The branch was burning back toward him. He leapt to the ground. And there, he felt the fire. As Uncle Will said, it burned underground. Ossie had to get out. Emma wasn't here and he shouldn't be. He raced across the fiery earth and branches fell from every tree. He took one path, then another, and the fire always found him.

Ossie did not know, could not know that Emma was among that thick animal crowd, *looking for him.*

The swamp rat reached water, a slough's small inlet, surrounded by burning forest. Wildfire was behind him, in front. A bay tree burst to flame. Fire was above him, too, in the red whipping wind, burning and churning the air.

He jumped to the water, through a mud-thick cover of ash, into brown darkness. Even underwater, he could see the fire. Its light crackled through the shadowy water. Below him was nothing. He would go there if he could. He would wait far under the water.

But he couldn't. He came to the surface to breathe. And there was no air.

The water itself had caught fire.

CHAPTER 30

IN THE BEAST'S BELLY

A fiery wind whipped past and Ossie found air and took what he could. He realized then how tired he was as he treaded water, arms and legs like stone. Above him, the smoke parted and he saw the whole burning sky. He could not move. Then, in the red rolling flames, he saw something else. . . .

It wasn't clear at first. The smoke stung his eyes and blur was all he saw. He looked again and it was his family. They moved freely in the burning air. They were forms drawn in flame, shapes etched in ember. He saw his father, his mother, his sisters and brothers.

When the snake had first come, he had been a small child. Before this, he could not remember his family. He kept a hazy memory of his mother and father, but the brothers and sisters had long since faded to a single face, a sound, a smell, a sense.

But here they were and he knew each one, once more. Over the fire's roar, he heard them—voices from a rush of flame.

His mother seemed to call him. *Ossie.*

His brothers and sisters ran, played, chased, fought. *Come on, Ossie! This way!*

His father was trying to tell him something, too. Ossie listened, close. *Don't be scared, boy.*

And he wasn't. The fire moved over the water, toward him. He let himself drift toward them. . . .

But then something stopped him.

"Where're you headin off to?" came another voice through the deafening fire.

Ossie saw two eyes in the ashy water and a thousand fires reflected across them.

It was Uncle Will. "Tell em not yet. Tell em you're not ready to go with em."

Ossie said, "I'm tired, Uncle Will."

The swamp rat looked up. His family was gone. Uncle Will said, "You and me both."

Ossie climbed onto Will's shoulder and they moved quickly to the far edge of the fire. There were places where the smoke and flame were thick and Will had to move underwater and streaks of orange firelight swam with them. Ossie held on tight.

Uncle Will took him to the Piney Wood. The shore was lined, two dozen deep, with swamp folk watching their old home burn. Ossie saw Emma and went over toward her. Her mother and father said nothing, but they took Emma with them. Ossie stayed where he was.

Nobody had seen Mr. Took.

• • •

The fire burned the rest of that night and half the next day. Then a peculiar wind blew from the south and the fire turned to follow it. The swamp folk watched it move away across the plain and they watched until it was a small rise of smoke in the distance.

When the land cooled, a few of them went to see what the fire had left. Will took Ossie, Preacher flew, and a few others came along.

Everything was black and charred and warm. There was a heavy dark smell on the place, but Will and Preacher were pleased.

"Fire was movin too fast to do much harm," said Will. "Burned into the ground some, but not too deep."

"Most of these here trees should be just fine," Preacher said.

Still, it would take a good rain to put things right. A caracara bird wandered past. "Good mornin, gentlemen, good mornin!"

Ossie heard Preacher whisper to himself, very low, "Good for you, you morbid thing."

"Hello," said Will to the bird.

Preacher put on a smile and said, "Howdy, friend."

The bird smiled back, big, bright. "Lovely day! Haven't seen such a lovely day since I can't remember when!"

Preacher nodded, polite. The caracara headed on, still talking about what a lovely, lovely day it was. Preacher shuddered and muttered, "You morbid thing," once more.

Will told Ossie, "That's Brother Caracara. He shows up after fires, lookin for the little folk who didn't make it. He likes the taste of burned grubs."

"Morbid thing," Preacher said again and shuddered again.

At least, Ossie thought to himself, Emma was allright.

A few trees didn't live. Fire got the roots of some younger ones. In time they rotted, in time they fell. The swamp folk stayed away during this. They lived in the Piney Wood and these were strange and strained times.

About a week went by and then a slow steady wind started to blow. It smelled of a burned forest and all that the swamp had been. The Prophet Bubba came flying back on this wind.

CHAPTER 31
IN THE PINEY WOOD

No one was happy. No one was home.

As days went by, more folk showed up. They'd been run out, too, and the forest here grew crowded. With so many in a small place, there wasn't much of anything to go around.

They got edgy and edgier, until it seemed there was some argument, somewhere, all the time. Trees were filled with birds in shrill fights over whose branch was whose. Things were no better on the forest floor. If an armadillo went digging for food, there was a raccoon to say this spot was his, thank-you-now-get-out-of-here.

Self-fragmentized, that's what they were.

None of the fights were bad, nobody got hurt, but it was always loud. Ossie heard a box turtle and a night heron shouting, calling names, insulting each other's family, many generations back. Ossie wondered if he should stop it, if he *could* stop it.

He wondered again about the Unspoken Word. If there was such a thing, shouldn't they hear it now? Could they need it more than now?

Or maybe it was no such Word. Maybe it was only another swamp legend. . . .

Ossie hadn't seen Emma since the fire and he went looking for her. He was moving quietly through the pines when he heard two birds talking. One was Blue Pete, the kingfisher. The other was the Prophet Bubba. They hadn't seen him.

"Listen to me," Bubba was saying.

"I'm listenin," Blue Pete said, "but I don't like what I hear."

"I tell you, it's the rat-child."

Ossie stopped, quiet.

"Come on now, Mr. Bubba. Let's not be sayin such things."

"I wouldn't, Blue Pete, less I knowed it was true."

The kingfisher let out a long slow whistle.

And the Prophet Bubba went on, "Wildfire came cause of that creature. And the fire's gonna come back—maybe not today or tomorrow or six months hence. But it's gonna come back! Until we do somethin about the swamp rat, we'll *never* be safe!"

Ossie went to find Emma. He went on anyway. And as he went, he did not notice the Fall turn to Winter.

PART FOUR

THE RIVER WIDE & PURE

CHAPTER 32
SKEETERS

Fish don't swim in a dry Swamp.
—a swamp saying

It was early afternoon when he found her and he didn't tell her what he'd heard that Winter morning—what the Prophet had been saying.

But he didn't have to. Her own parents were saying it. Emma slipped away with him and they went through the Piney Wood and as they went they talked.

They made plans. They'd run away, the two of them. They'd get the others to come along. Gib, Tudd, Stubb, Lodemia, Philomena, *the mouse,* anybody who wanted in, not counting Johnny. They'd set out together and find an island and it would be theirs. They'd start from scratch, this little group. They'd make a whole new world and theirs would work better than this.

They made big plans. Of course they didn't believe any of it for a fast second.

Maybe it was because they were talking, maybe that's why they didn't hear. They should have heard that exceptional sound. It was a Mosquito Song, led by the Great King Zed.

Ossie and Emma passed under some close-growing palmettos, into a widening with a small pond in the center. The ground opened deep through the pocked rock, and the pond was filled by an underground spring. It had no bottom to speak of.

The mosquitoes alone knew about this secret water treasure. And they were keeping it for themselves.

Swamp folk thought the mosquitoes had died out in the drought. They thought the mosquitoes had dried up and blown away like dust. Nobody had seen one in months. And it was because they were here. In this pond. Every last one of the worthless little demons.

The Great King Zed kept his mosquito-tribe swarming above the pond, day and night, warning off trespassers with a greedy grasping whine. There were more mosquitoes here than stars in the night sky. The air was thick with them, brown like mud with them. They shaded the sun and made the ground dark as dusk.

When Ossie and Emma happened on them, King Zed called for his tribe to attack, to protect their sacred water, to fight to the death! The rats were bitten again and again, around the ears, eyes, hundreds, thousands of the things lit on them, biting, biting. Ossie thought they might carry him away and Emma, too. The mosquitoes' drilling buzz was loud as thunder. They were like water, rushing, pouring over the rats and biting, biting, biting.

Zed cheered his tribe, stirring them to frenzy. It was chaos, a riot, worse every second, as more and more joined in, biting, biting, biting the swamp rats. Ossie batted at them, bit at them, smashed them under his feet. But King Zed only called for more of them. And more of them came.

Emma screamed and Ossie called for her to "Run!"

"Run where?"

"Anywhere!"

He found a break in the scrub palm and led Emma as best he could, one way, then another.

A fog of the demons clung to the two rats. Ossie had heard stories of madness and death under a swarming of mosquitoes. They said the endless stinging sent folk running through the swamp until they dropped and the mosquitoes drained them of lifeblood, leaving them dead and flat and dry as an old leaf. It wasn't the way Ossie wanted to go, flat, dry, leaf-like.

He kept Emma moving on a zigging, zagging course and suddenly the mosquitoes were gone.

The swamp rats never knew the reason.

The mosquitoes had ended the chase when word reached them: The Great Zed was dying, gravely injured when Ossie stepped on him. The tribe found him near death, lying in a pool of stolen blood. He was weak, but managed these last words.

"When the Songs . . . the Songs are sung . . . of the Great . . . the Great King Zed . . . let them say . . . he died nobly . . . and for noble cause . . ."

And then he was gone from them.

As it turned out, there were no songs. The others forgot him by that afternoon. If you ask a mosquito today, he will not know of this fallen leader. Mosquitoes have no sense of history. These are the only words you're ever likely to hear of the Great King Zed.

Ossie and Emma stopped. Their faces were swollen with bites, speckled with blood. Emma scratched and Ossie said, "Wait." He smelled at the air. He knew what they needed. "Come on," he said.

He found a stream, long since dry, and dug until he found moist soil. A little deeper was warm mud. He told Emma to cover her bites with it and she did. It took away the sting. Ossie helped her, wiped mud behind her ears, carefully near her eyes. She was better now.

He looked to see where they were. But he didn't know. They'd come so far, they were out of the Piney Wood and into the Devil's Garden.

Or at least he thought. This place was unfamiliar to him and Emma, too. The drought was even worse here, a whole world turning to dust. The small rats were thirsty, but there was no water to drink. They set out to find their way back to the others as the sun climbed higher and grew hotter. Ossie knew they couldn't go much farther without drink.

The little rats moved slowly on and passed the colorless shells of six turtles, gathered close in a circle, two big ones, four little ones, a whole family lost to the drought. They saw the tangled bones of fish, picked over by birds. And the sun grew hotter still.

. . .

By late afternoon, the swamp rats were in trouble and they knew it. They needed water. They needed to drink and to rest.

But there was nothing. There was no shade, there were no plants left. Ossie and Emma kept on. Once they caught a smell of water, but never came to it.

Within an hour, they stopped again. They could not go on any farther.

They huddled close together and soon they drifted off. Ossie never felt sleep come over him. But the next he knew, two turkey buzzards were there, on either side, young birds, no older than he was, feathers dark like a moonless night.

Ossie quickly woke Emma. One of the buzzards looked at them with a small puzzled eye. "How you two doin?"

"Not real good," Ossie answered. He helped Emma up and they started walking again, not fast. The buzzards walked alongside them, with slow loping walks.

"Lot of folk aren't doin real good these days," the other buzzard said.

"Course, *we* are doin okay. Even better than okay. Us buzzards are doin *real* good," the first bird said, a small laugh.

The swamp rats kept on and one buzzard said to other, "Guess we oughta tell the folks bout these two."

"The folks will be tickled, won't they?" the other said. Then he told Ossie and Emma, "Not that we specially enjoy doin this, but we got to."

The swamp rats said nothing.

"Let's not lie to these kids," one bird said to the other. "We *do* specially enjoy it!"

The first buzzard laughed. "True, true! You got me there, brother! We do indeed!"

"We downright love it!" the second one said. "We're lucky that way. We love what we do!"

"And we do what we love!"

The buzzards shared a loud cackling laugh over that.

"We hope you'll unnerstan!"

Ossie said, "We hope you'll unnerstan if we don't unnerstan."

The buzzards flew off, their laughter echoing over the dry plain. Ossie wished that Will were here now, he wished that someone could help him find the way back.

But they were alone and there was little time left to them.

It wasn't long before the rest came, a dozen buzzards, circling, piled high on the clouds, a lot of them for two small rats. Maybe things weren't so good for these birds as they pretended.

Ossie and Emma kept going. They would not lie down for the buzzards. Ossie knew the birds would wait, up there, circling and circling, for days if they had to. "Patient as a buzzard," that's what Will used to say.

Then Ossie saw something move and it moved closer. It moved in jerky fits, sidewise, then forward, a painful crooked path. In another second, he saw. It was a rat snake, the one Ossie had seen at the egret nest so long ago, the one who was knocked out of the tree. He'd gotten pretty bent-up in that fall. Emma saw it, too.

The rat snake looked thin and hungry. Ossie wondered if he'd remember, or just eat and give them no thought.

Ossie couldn't run, could only watch. The snake kept coming. And what would the buzzards think about this? Maybe there would be a fight. Over who got to eat the swamp rats.

That would be worth seeing. Even if it was the last thing they saw.

Then Emma saw something else, farther off. "Ossie," she whispered. "Do you see that?"

He looked and he saw. "I . . . I think so. . . ."

But it wasn't really there, was it? It wasn't a thing. It was more like a dream let loose on the face of the swamp. Whatever it was, it moved quickly. It drifted just above the dried prairie. And then, in one impossible moment, it was there.

It was an Indian, a young boy, alone. But in another moment, there were more. There were five and they were children. They wore bright-colored clothes, their skin deep brown like the swamp water had once been, their hair a dark black. They were around the swamp rats now, looking down on them.

Ossie knew these were the Children of the Sun, like Rufus had told about. "It's allright," he said quietly to Emma. "Don't be afraid."

They watched as one of the Children, a little girl, picked up the rat snake. "What'd I do! Leave me be! A snake's got needs, you know!" The rat snake bit her arm, again and again. But the child didn't care. She took it to a place by the trees and set it down. She shooed it off with no words. Another child waved his arms and the buzzards cleared from the sky. Now they knelt by the swamp rats. Other Children picked them up and covered them with their hands. It was cool there and dark. In an instant, the rats were asleep.

When they woke, they were on cracked ground again, only feet from a small running channel. They crawled to the water and drank. Ossie knew where he was. He knew this part of the swamp. They weren't far from Big Cypress.

The two of them lay by the water, wondering, trying to understand. Had it happened? Had the Children been there? Or had they both dreamed it together? Had they stumbled to water on their own?

The more they thought, the more they knew they'd never know.

Now you ask, how do I know this happened? It was so far from here.

Didn't I mention? Birds tell me things. Brother Crow sometimes stops in Devil's Garden and he was there that day. He saw it happen, he told me.

Maybe he didn't tell me to my face. Sometimes birds don't remember to tell me things. They are forgetful creatures. But I was under the earth and the crow was talking right above. And if he didn't say these things to me, that doesn't make them less true.

It really doesn't.

Two days had passed since Ossie and Emma had left. But as soon as they came upon the others, they saw that something was wrong. Everyone was running everywhere, nowhere, calling to families, gathering children.

Ossie and Emma heard. It had happened to a family of mice. Three children and a grandfather had been lost. No one saw it, but four mice were gone, sure as that. The other mice were crying, wailing.

Mr. Took had been there. The old rattler was back.

Ossie asked, "Which mice did he get? Is *the mouse* okay?"

"*What* mouse?" *"the mouse"* was all he knew, so he never got an answer.

When Emma's family found her, they grabbed her and shook her: *Where have you been? Why did you leave? What were you doin? What were you thinkin?* They saw Ossie. *Was he with you? Did you go with him!* They were sure the snake had got her. They took her away and Ossie went to find Uncle Will.

The old gator was with Preacher, where a shallow channel still ran. Ossie watched the swamp folk running, scattering, shattering into small clustered groups. He said, "Wouldn't we be safer, all of us keepin close together? We could warn each other if Mr. Took came back."

Will nodded again. "Why don't you tell em?"

"Me? How would I? How could I? What would I say?"

"Same as you told us," Preacher said.

"But," said Ossie, "what if they don't want to hear it?"

And Will said, "What if they do?"

They listened. But they didn't listen long. Ossie could not convince them. "We're on our own," they said, "each family looks out for its own self." Possums went one way, armadillos another, and that was how it had to be, they said.

CHAPTER 33

THE LAST DREAM

As goes the Gator, so the Swamp goes.
These are the words of the Master of Breath,
Who walks the Path from birth to Death.
          —from "The Song of the Swamp"

S o Ossie crossed the Piney Wood alone. For hour after
hour he went on, looking, watching out. Even as the
others slept, he went and watched. He was careful, cautious. The snake could be anywhere. He passed the makeshift
nest where Emma lived and it was quiet. Stubb and the other
turtles slept closed in their shells, snores echoing out. Ossie
happened across *the mouse* and his family, asleep and well.
Clavis and his brothers and sister quietly followed their father,
slowly through the trees. Each family kept to its own.

Ossie circled the forest and came back and found Uncle

Will. He was in another heavy sleep. Ossie settled nearby and watched, very quiet.

Half the night passed that way. Ossie thought on many things, where he was and where he'd been, and where he might go. He looked at the old gator sleeping and thought about all Will had done for him and that's when he noticed. Uncle Will was old. He was older than old. He was the most ancient thing there was. He was from some other time. Ossie didn't like it, but that was what it was. Uncle Will was old.

Another hour more, and Will woke up. Ossie was there still. The gator had been in another of his Dreams. He told it to Ossie. And it was this.

Life and the Swamp were born of the sea. There was a time before life and a time before the Swamp. In the beginnin there was Ocean and the Land was still to be.

Then, over long ages, the sea drew back. A rocky flat place appeared, risin from the floor of that great Ocean. The water ran from it and the Gator was here and he saw. This was Land, with no shape to it. A wide river ran across it. In time, sawgrass plains rose from the water of the river. And in that grass was seed for more grass. There were trees and plants of every kind, all with seed to grow more like em. And the Gator was here and he saw.

And then came the Swamp Folk, every kind, those that walked the Earth and birds that filled the Sky and fish that swam the River. And this was the Swamp. If you had been just one drop of Water, it would take you a year to move from one end to the other. It was as big as that.

The Gator was here and he saw. This was the Swamp and everythin in it—and the swamp is a River of water and the river of Water is Life.

Now Will's dreams had taken him back as far as he could go. He saw what the first gator saw and there was nothing beyond that. He sat and watched the drying swamp. And the drought did strange and horrible things.

Over the days and weeks that followed, the swamp finished drying. There were few running streams now. The drier it got, the hotter it got. There were no clouds to muffle the sun and it tortured the land. Rufus had long ago gone, swimming up a disappearing river in search of deep water. When Will went to feed, he had to cross wide places of dust, no sawgrass to hide him. Many of the swamp folk had left altogether and there were no birds to warn Will of danger. On this day, Ossie stayed close in by the rat-lodge. There were no sounds in the swamp. Even the bugs were silent.

Anyway, no sound would move far in that heavy air. Ossie didn't hear five shots from two guns.

Later, with afternoon almost done, Will had still not returned. Ossie was used to it. The gator often went for long stretches. Especially now, with the swamp dry, finding food was hard. Will had to go farther each time.

But this time the Poachers found him.

When Will did come back, Ossie didn't see anything wrong. Maybe the gator seemed a little more tired. Maybe he moved a little more slowly. Maybe his voice had a strange raw rasp in it.

Then Ossie saw the wounds in his side. Uncle Will told him the story.

He had been heading across a dry field, toward a cypress

stand. He hadn't seen the two Men there, waiting. They were quiet. Will was almost on them when they jumped. Both shot at the same time. They were right on top of him and he couldn't get away. And they couldn't get away from him. At least, Will said, there were two fewer Poachers in the world.

At first, Ossie was sure the gator would get better. The wounds seemed trifling. But by the next day, there were changes. Will hardly moved, only to keep up with the shade. His voice was more raw and raspier still. There was nothing Ossie could do to help.

By the second afternoon, Will looked bad. He hadn't spoken for half the day.

Then he said, "I better get goin."

"Goin where?" Ossie asked.

Will was getting up and saying, "To find out what's past the mangroves."

Ossie only said, "Don't leave." He only said, "Don't."

But Will kept going and the swamp rat followed, silent. After a time Will stopped. He said, "You don't need to be out here, boy. Go back to em. You know the way."

The gator moved across the cracked dry mud and Ossie watched until he was gone. The swamp rat stayed there, not daring to move.

CHAPTER 34

EVENING SONG

It was night. Ossie watched the sky. Thin ragged clouds confused the darkness. The world was as still and quiet as he was.

Until there rose an impossible sound, slowly, over the whole swamp. It was a great deep bellowing. It came from every corner, the mournful grunted bellow of a thousand alligators. It rose like Song, and the air was filled with it.

Suddenly Preacher was beside Ossie. He hadn't heard the bird fly in. "That'd be Will's children," the old heron said.

Ossie was amazed. He'd never heard of any children.

"Will must have a hunnert children spread round this swamp," the Preacher went on.

Ossie was still more amazed.

"He used to go see em all the time, the times he left you places, the times you were off with friends and what-all. He'd go check on em, see how their lives were progressin. He'd help em through bad times and enjoy the good times with em. Will outlived their mothers, outlived some of the children, too. But there's a bunch of em out there, a bunch of Will's children. Wasn't sure if you knew that."

The swamp rat nodded now, it was good to know. Preacher nodded back and flew off.

But Ossie stayed. He stayed long into the night. The bellows stopped after a while. And after a while longer, he heard someone call to him from a distance.

He thought it was Preacher again. He answered, "What is it?" There was no reply, only another call. "Preacher?" But there was nothing more. There was silence.

"Who's there?" he asked, and again there was no answer.

He heard the call once more. And he understood. It was no voice. It was wind.

The wind grew stronger as it crossed the swamp. It blew onto Ossie and in it he smelled the warmth of water that was no longer there. He smelled fresh shoots of sawgrass that grew no more. He felt the seasons and smelled each plant, each creature in the world, every last thing. The wind tore the clouds from the sky, scrubbed it clean, and a bottomless night opened above him. Ossie saw a star streak by, dropping, sparkling, from the sky. And then it was gone. He knew the old alligator was dead.

He listened to the wind and he cried.

CHAPTER 35

NOT FIT FOR A BUZZARD

When the swamp folk found out, they had stories about Will. The ibis, the egrets, raccoons, squirrels, all of them had stories. In every story they were each his good friend. Not one had been scared of him, had shied away from him. He was the one you could trust, they said. Never mind the Prophet, it was Will you looked to for answers. Those were the things they said.

It bothered Ossie for a while, hearing it. Then he wasn't sure it mattered. The swamp has short memory for things such as you and me, he thought. The swamp has bigger things on its mind.

A lot more folk had left now. The water was gone. There was talk of a full slough, miles away, but the only water here was that one slight stream, no wider than a tree, not water enough for a family of snails.

The fields were dirt. The brittle stalks of dead sawgrass were gone, scattered by wind. Trees were dying and smaller hammocks had disappeared altogether.

Some turtles buried themselves, digging for cool moisture. Whether they found it, no one knew. Others never made it that far. Their empty shells, chalky white, littered the prairies of dust. Most birds had left. There were no fish to eat. The nights weren't filled with frog-song. The frogs had not lived.

For weeks and months, the buzzards feasted. Dead things were everywhere.

But no more. Even the buzzards grew thin. They suffered. Some died. No one had known a time as dry as this.

The swamp was dying and everything in it.

And then Ossie remembered. He remembered what Will told him. He remembered the Gator Hole, Will's island. He didn't know if it was still there. But it might be. It could be. He'd have to go. If there was water, he could take the others. Maybe this time they'd listen. It was a long way, a day's walk, maybe more, and in the heat. There would be nothing to hide him, to keep him safe from the birds.

But the swamp wasn't fit for buzzards now. He wouldn't have to worry. He waited till First Dark, when the sun had gone, and he went. He was tired and thirsty and hadn't eaten for a while. The bugs were gone, too, and rats went hungry. He made his way slowly, careful not to over-tire himself.

He walked through that night and the next morning he stopped under a gumbo-limbo tree. It was dead from drought, but there was shade. He rested through the heat of that day. As the sun went again, he started again.

On the morning of the third day, he saw it. In the shattered swamp, it was a place of brilliant green. Every tree, every vine, every flower was living, fed by the water of Will's pond. He hurried, running. Under the canopy of thick trees, the island air was cool. The fields of wood sage bloomed and no one else was there. It was a secret still.

He found the pond as full as ever. The whole place was as it had been. He drank the cold water and he slept.

The ground was damp here, full of bugs. Ossie ate, then slept again. When the sun set, he started back to the others. Maybe this time, they would listen. With his stomach full, the trip was easier. But things did not go as he hoped.

CHAPTER 36

DONE IN

While Ossie was gone, Bubba got busy. The Prophet Bubba started laying down rules. With Will out of the way, there was nobody to tell him not to. Bubba laid down rules, rules for this, rules for that, rules, rules, and more rules! There were rules saying who could do what and when. There were rules about who would have water. And who would go without.

Of course Ossie didn't know about any of this, not yet. As soon as he got back, he tried to tell everyone about the island. He told Emma's family. There was water for them all, he said, and plenty of food. But Emma's father only moved on, like he wasn't even there. Emma turned to him as they left. "I'm sorry," is what she said.

Wherever he went, it was the same. Clavis's family ignored

him. Gib's father wouldn't talk to him. Others hurried away as soon as they saw him coming.

The swamp rat went to Preacher. Maybe Preacher could tell them. But Preacher knew it was no use. No one would listen, not to Ossie, not to him. By now, the swamp folk blamed the rat for their troubles. They were sure this talk of a secret island, of a full deep pond, was some trick he was playing on them. They did not trust him. Bubba had made sure of that.

Ossie found a branch and sat. It seemed, as he sat, that he'd done nothing with all Will taught him. He'd come to understand the swamp in a lot of ways, and it did him no good.

Preacher joined him. "Let me tell you, boy," the old heron said, right off. "You can't change the basic way folk basically are."

Ossie didn't say anything.

"There's a sayin in the swamp and it says this. A fish only swims in so much water. Y'unnerstan?"

"No."

"Well, then. What it means is this. A fish swims in a pond, and the pond feeds off a channel, and the channel runs to a river, and the river drains to the sea, and what-all. Now y'unnerstan?"

"No," Ossie said again.

Preacher hmphed a time or two. "It means the fish don't know how much water is around him. See, he's in a pond that's really part of a far bigger thing. But that doesn't matter to the fish. Cause the fish only swims in so much water. Y'unnerstan now."

"No."

"Well," Preacher said. And he stopped. And he said,

"Come to think of it, I don't either." He stomped his feet out. "Fish only swims in so much water! It's a dumb sayin, that's what it is!"

Preacher was quiet for a while, then, "This is a dry time, son. It's rough on folk. Tends to make em a little in-directed. A little . . . self-fragmentized. If you see what I mean."

"Yeah, Preacher," said Ossie. "I see what you mean."

CHAPTER 37

BUBBA READS THE SIGNS

Will knows the Swamp like no one else; he knows it in full and
in part,
He knows each last Mosquito by name and what's in a
Rattlesnake heart,
He's a friend to every Bird that's flown, he can tell you the
mood of a Tree,
Cause Will knows that the Swamp is a puzzle, and the pieces
are You & Me.

—from "The Song of the Swamp"

I f it wasn't bad enough—and it was—Bubba made sure it
got worse. He went to River Otter and said, "I have a question. Maybe you can help."

River Otter raised up and nodded, oh, of course. He'd be
proud to. "What is your question, sir?"

"When did our Troubles begin?"

Raccoon came by about then and stopped to see what was going on.

"Our Troubles . . . ," River Otter started off, trying hard to think. "Um, the exact day, is that what you mean, sir?"

The Prophet Bubba nodded. "Yessir. The preeecise day."

"Well, I believe it was, uh . . . must've been around . . . roughly, oh . . . on or about . . ." River Otter had a little coughing fit, embarrassed to admit he did not know the answer.

A crowd was quickly gathering. Bubba waited till it was good-sized, then he said, "Listen to me! Our Troubles began the day the Swamp Rat was *born*! When he come among us, he brung Sufferin upon us!"

It happened that Preacher was wandering by and he saw what was going on. "What-all we talkin bout?" he asked, knowing full well.

"The swamp rat! Ossie!" Gib's father called this out.

Preacher found an old log to stand on, making himself just higher than Bubba. "We settled all that. That's yesterday's news."

"But the Trouble is with us *today*!" someone yelled.

Preacher was about to speak, but Bubba hopped higher in the tree and called out, "Ossie made the Drought—and he called the Fire on us—and he tells the Serpent what to do and when and to who!"

Preacher laughed loud and long and said, "Bubba, tell us you're jokin."

"Preacher," the Prophet answered softly, "this is no joke."

"Have you lost what-all sense you had!" Preacher called out, spat out. But the rest of them were muttering and murmuring. Ossie was making it happen, Prophet said he was.

"Folks," said Preacher, "let's not take leave of our senses. Let's not get *self-fragmentized*!" He gave them a quick sideways look to see how they took to the word. They didn't seem to care for it.

"This is nothin but a little dry spell!" called Preacher. "We've been through worse!" He called to a gator. "Tyrell, you remember! You remember ten years back! Got so dry, the air cracked!"

But Tyrell turned away from Preacher. "Wasn't bad as this."

Preacher tried to speak again, but they all spoke over him. "Never been this bad," they were saying. "Things were allright till he came." "He's the cause." "He's behind it." "Ain't no hope for us now."

"Listen to me!" Bubba shouted. "There *is* hope if you listen to me!"

And they listened.

"We can overcome this," the Prophet went on, *"if—you—come—together—and—together—you do—as I say!"*

The swamp folk were yelling now, cheering now. Preacher might as well not have been there. He went to find Ossie before the rest of them did.

CHAPTER 38

EMMA

Ossie wasn't surprised when Preacher told him. He wondered it himself. Maybe everything *was* his fault. Maybe he *had* brought the troubles on them.

He would leave. This time for good.

Ossie would leave and he would not come back to this place, not ever again. It might help them. But there was one thing he had to do first.

He waited for night.

There was no moon, no stars, not a firefly in the forest. It was as dark as Ossie had ever seen it. He moved quietly through the smothering night, off to say good-bye to Emma.

He didn't want to be seen, but a time or two, he almost was. He heard a pair of possum walking a trail toward him. He hopped in a tree. And there, moving branch to branch, he nearly walked into an egret's legs. But the bird was sleeping and did not wake.

He reached the quickly built nest where Emma was staying. He heard her family and they were talking about him. He slipped closer in the night, hardly breathing, moving shadow to shadow.

He was lucky. Emma was off from the rest of them, alone. He called to her, no more than a whisper, and she heard. She left with him.

They began to talk, out in the blinding dark, and before Ossie could tell her, Emma said, "We're leavin."

"Why?"

"Cause of the Prophet. He said it's time to move. He said we got to go someplace where you aren't. He said the Unspoken Word said so."

"Did it?" asked Ossie.

"I don't know," she told him.

"Did *you* hear it, Emma?"

"No," she answered. "I didn't."

"I didn't either," said Ossie.

"But Bubba told everybody. Said *he* heard it."

"He's a full-blown flat-out fool, you know that," said Ossie.

"I know, but a lot of em don't. And I can't make em see."

"Where's he want you to move?"

"Someplace where there's water and food," said Emma.

"There's only one place like that. Will's Island. I tried to tell em. We could've shown em the way, but nobody would listen."

Emma nodded.

"They'll only find another dry place, a new dry place," Ossie said.

She could only shrug. There was nothing she could do to change the things that were.

"Tell your father to wait, Emma. At least a little while."

"He won't."

"If he waits, things might get better. They might."

"Why?" she asked.

"Cause *I'm* leavin," he told her. "Tell your father and maybe it'll make a difference to him."

"I don't understand, Ossie. Why are you goin?"

"It might help."

"How? None of it's your fault."

"I know, or I guess. But if I wasn't here, they'd have less to argue about. Maybe they could figure some things out. Pull together some. If they make it till the rains come . . ."

Emma shook her head. "It might help," Ossie said again and that's when they jumped him. Johnny and his rat-friends jumped him. He hadn't heard them coming, neither had Emma. It was a bad fight, and this time, Ossie was outnumbered. This time, he was tired. This time, the rats got the best of him.

He was knocked, bitten, scratched, bruised, beaten. When he tried to fight back, he had no chance. Johnny and his friends were all over him. Emma was yelling, loud, and her father came running. Others came running, too. But not one tried to stop the fight.

The Prophet Bubba watched from high in a tree and he was mightily pleased.

Emma pulled her brother off, but the others kept on until

Ossie wasn't moving. They left him there, dirty, bleeding. They left, all but Emma. Ossie got up, slowly.

"Are you allright?" she asked.

"Well, I've been better," he said, and he headed out of the scrub forest.

CHAPTER 39

OSSIE'S LAST JOURNEY

He didn't go far that first night. He was tired and hurt and wanted to rest. He waited for morning and then he left the Piney Wood. With the dawning sun came a long slow wind. It moved over the dead prairies and across Ossie as he walked. In it was the smell of a rotting dead land.

For a minute he tried to outrun it. But he was too tired and he stopped and walked with it. Dusty muck rolled alongside him.

He didn't know where he was going, but he went. He would never be lost again, because he had nowhere to go.

The sun was up and hot and Ossie was crossing a wide stretch, the waterless bottom of a waterless slough. He'd crossed this place many times, with Uncle Will. And suddenly he saw.

This was the place the hyacinth had been. It was that part of the journey he always forgot. The place that was new to him every time. He'd forgotten it again, and again it was new. It was lifeless now, nothing but the ghost-shadow of plants.

He was halfway across when he saw the snake. It was there, behind a dusty mound. It was Mr. Took and Mr. Took was glad to see him. The snake looked healthy and happy.

"Is it my friend again, the swamp rat?" he said in his ugly jagged voice.

Ossie didn't answer.

"You look terrible, you mind my sayin?" the snake said. It was true, the rattler was better off than Ossie.

"I don't mind," the swamp rat said.

The snake moved himself a little closer. "I've been thinkin, haven't I, and what I thought was this. I should've ate you long ago, shouldn't I? It's time to set things right, don't you think?"

Ossie was tired and hurt from the fight, but the thought of Mr. Took getting him was too much. He started running. And Mr. Took went after him. There was a dry island ahead, in a dry lake, and there were trees on it. If Ossie could get to one, he could get away from the snake.

But he wasn't going to make it. Another few feet on, he stumbled in the soft soil and his leg twisted. He got up, limping, and the snake would be on him in a second.

Ossie stopped running and waited for Mr. Took.

"That's much better, ain't it?" the snake said. "Now things'll finally be as they was meant to be, won't they?"

He started to coil, rising up. His mouth was open and his

THE TALE OF THE SWAMP RAT

poison dripped from each fang and it glistened in the blistering sun.

Before I forget, there's another thing. We have to leave Ossie, running from the snake, because there's more to the story. It started this same morning, back in the Piney Wood.

The Prophet Bubba called everyone together. "The time has come," he told them. "I have heard the Unspoken Word and it has told me to lead you from the swamp *now*."

Emma's family was there. They were in a dry field of palmetto and Bubba said things would be good soon. They would find water in a new land. They were free of the curse, they had rid themselves of the swamp rat. They only had to follow him now. "All of us goes but the swamp rat," Bubba said. The Prophet called for them to start, and they did.

All except Emma.

Her mother called, a whisper. "Emma!"

The Prophet Bubba saw and said, "Move along, young miss. You can't hold up a thing as grand as this."

Her father turned and heard her say, "I'm not goin. I'll stay here."

Her parents couldn't believe it, not from Emma. Johnny, they might have expected. But not Emma. "Emma!" her father hollered. He had never raised his voice to her till now. "Emma!" a second time.

"I'm old enough," she said. "I can stay alone."

And before they could speak, Tudd was saying, "Me, too."

"Tudd?" his father said. "What you talkin bout, boy?"

"If Ossie's not goin," the armadillo answered, "I'm not goin either."

And now another voice. "I'm stayin with em." It was Gib the owl and he meant it.

The Prophet Bubba looked to the mothers and fathers to get the youngsters in line. But even as he waited for that to happen, more of them spoke up. "I'm not goin if they're not goin," said the possum Clavis. The Quail-Sisters said it, too. And *the mouse* and the other swamp rats.

"Hullo," came a voice. "Name's Stubb and I'm stayin." He was moving, slowly, to join his friends.

Stubb's father looked to Stubb's mother. "Well, Myrna? What do you say?"

She nodded. "I say we stay." And they followed Stubb.

The father said, "Never much liked that bird," as they passed Bubba.

The color went from the Prophet Bubba, from his feathers, from his old iron head. "Now, hold on!" he yelled. "Listen to me! LISTEN TO ME!"

They listened. But for the very first time in his very long life, Bubba did not know what to say.

The old rattler was smiling, big and wide. It was over now, all over, and the snake had won.

Ossie was tired and ready for it to end.

Mr. Took pulled back and struck. But even as he did, he stopped. He was only an inch from Ossie and there came a confused look to his eye.

Ossie was confused, too.

And then he saw. "Mornin, Ossie," said Brother Bear. The bear had come from nowhere and now he had a paw planted on Mr. Took, just behind the head. The snake couldn't reach the swamp rat. Mr. Took whipped and fought and twisted, but couldn't get free of the bear.

A butterfly had led the way to the swamp rat, following dusty tracks through the dusty swamp.

"Hurry up, Tim Junior," came another voice now.

"I'm comin, Tom Junior," came still another.

Two wasps flew past and stung Mr. Took.

"Uh-oh, Tim Junior," said Tom Junior. "Don't s'pose we should've done that."

"Oh, Tom Junior," said Tim Junior, "course we should've." The snake squirmed harder.

"Mornin, Ossie," said Blue Pete as he flew in and jabbed his sharp beak into Mr. Took's side.

Tudd and his family came now, crawling out of the forest and over to attack the snake. The burrowing owls, Gib and his family, came, too. And the bear kept his foot on Mr. Took's head.

"Now is this . . . ," said Mr. Took, a strangled squeak, "is this the way it has to be?" It was the last question he ever asked.

Emma's family was there, and Clavis, Stubb, the Quail-Sisters, *the mouse*, every last one of them. Preacher flew in. Turtles and frogs appeared from under the soil. All of them scratched, bit, clawed, or stung that snake. Even the mosquitoes were there, a whole swarming load. Swamp folk poured from everywhere. No one wanted to be left out. They wanted to say they'd been there that day.

Ibis and egrets flew in. By a pond apple tree, Ossie saw Possum talking to Panther and they came over together. Hawk swooped down and joined Marsh Rabbit and together they attacked the snake.

• • •

I won't go into all that happened. But by the time it was done, there wasn't much left of Mr. Took. What there was, was in small pieces.

Ossie found Preacher and Preacher was beaming. "This is an exceptional day!"

The swamp folk congratulated each other, each claiming the idea was his. Each had got in the best hit, each was the one who did in Mr. Took.

That morning a cloud had settled over the swamp. It was pure and white and held no rain. It lifted now and an Unspoken Word passed among them. They all listened this time. They all heard it this time. Even Old Earlie who was stone deaf, she heard it. She heard it loud and clear: *"The swamp is a River of water and the river of Water is Life."* These are the words of the Master of Breath, who walks the Path from birth to Death.

The swamp folk understood, they had to find that Water again. And Ossie would lead them there. He knew the way.

As the sun rose to midday, they set out across the dry prairie in search of the river. Every creature remaining joined that line. It stretched, I would guess, a good half-mile. The little ones had trouble keeping up and Old Earlie needed help once. Stubb and his family made for the end of the line. But no one was left behind. They crossed what had been the broadest saw-grass plain, now a dusty wasted land. Ossie led them and Emma was with him.

They journeyed from the edge of this wilderness and came to a place with seventy royal palm, still holding to life. Ossie saw that the swamp folk were tired, so they rested. They gathered in the shade of the palms and when the sun began to fall, they set out again.

With the next morning, they saw it. Will's Island was before them, a wonderful dark green on the face of a dead swamp. Their clean long line fell apart then. They raced to the island, a fine chaos, and Ossie was glad.

The Gator Hole was deep with cool water, as Ossie knew it would be. There was plenty to go around. Panther drank next to Possum. Marsh Rabbit and Hawk stood side by side. They stayed there and the tired ones rested, the sick grew stronger, and the young grew older. The swamp might be dead, but on Will's Island things were good.

CHAPTER 40

CHANGE COMES ON A WIND

O ssie was among them when he realized, it turned out as Will knew. His pond had saved them and given life back to them. They stayed and things were good. On the morning of the seventh day, Ossie heard something. At first he took it to be an alligator's bellow. Or the bear's growl. He thought it might be a fight starting. He went looking and he went to the island's edge and found it. It was on the sawgrass plain. It was wind.

It was not just any wind. It was wind the swamp had not seen in a long time. It brought black mountains of cloud. The clouds hid each horizon, north to one end of the swamp, south to the other, to the earth and higher than Ossie could understand. There was nothing but cloud. This wind had brought a whole new sky.

The wind reached Ossie and it smelled of one thing and that one thing was rain.

He went to tell the others, but it had already started, they already knew. The pond rippled under it. With every new second, the rain only came harder. And then harder still. It pounded the island. Heavy drops tumbled through thick-grown cypress leaves. They headed for the island's edge and saw it happening.

Rain hit the dried muck and sent up puffing dust. The water disappeared into the earth. But soon the mud-cracks filled, a million tiny rivers. The rain grew heavier and puddles formed in low-lying channels.

Ossie suddenly saw what it meant. He got everyone hurrying. They had to get off the island, he said. They had to get home. The swamp would fill and the hammocks again float in a wide river. If they did not leave now, they would never get to their homes. Ossie and Emma and every family started walking, running, back. It rained that day and six more after. There was no pause in it. On their journey through that storm, not one of them was lost. Every last creature made it home, safe and happy.

Almost every last creature. It was peculiar, but in that storm—and it was a tremendous storm—there was only one single bolt of lightning. Just one. Just a quick one. And it hit the Prophet Bubba as he was resting on a tree limb. Split that tree right smack down the middle, fried it good. Bubba wasn't the same after that, not quite, not ever. He spent most days sitting on a stump, a bubbly stream of spittle dripping off his beak. "Listen to me," he'd say over and over, "listen to me." And nothing more than that.

Folk liked him better, this new Bubba.

When at last the rain stopped, the swamp was full once more.

The Resurrection Ferns were back and open and green. Within another week, sawgrass shoots appeared in wide pools. In time, the drought might never have been.

The swamp folk began their lives once more and none of them noticed that Winter was turning into Spring.

IT ENDS AS IT BEGAN

Many things happened that Spring and one I remember most. I was there to see it. It was late afternoon, heading toward First Dark. There were two little rats, a few weeks old, a boy and a girl, down among the roots of a cypress dead from drought or fire. The boy climbed and jumped and played and the girl watched.

"Come on!" the boy yelled.

And the girl only watched. She was shy and unsure and quiet. She had yet to speak a word and her parents wondered if she ever might. The Rat-Father found them and said, "We have to get home."

At the first, I didn't recognize Ossie. He had changed in a lot of ways. And in as many, he hadn't changed at all. The mark was mostly gone from his shoulder. He gathered his children and together with Emma they headed across the island.

Wherever they went in that swamp forest, there was always somebody calling out, "Lo, Ossie!"

"Hello, Blue Pete," he'd call back.

"Ossie! Over here! Clavis!"

The possum had a family of his own now, same as Gib and Tudd and *the mouse* and the quails, too.

"Hullo," came a voice. "Name's Stubb. And this here's Little Stubb, that's Littler Stubb, and yonder's Littlest Stubb. Children, say hullo to Ossie."

"Hullo," said the Stubbs.

And Ossie said hello and told his name and all his family's, too.

"Afternoon, Ossie!"

"Hello, Brother Bear."

To the children, it seemed their father knew everyone. It was near sunset and Ossie took his family up a tall cypress. The boy jumped limb to limb, sure he could do more than he could. They reached the top, where branches held back. A couple of young wasps flew around them.

"Hello," said one, "I'm—"

"Tim," said Ossie. "The other is Tom."

The wasps were amazed. "It's true!" one of them shouted.

"It's just as they say!" the other shouted, too. "Like in the Songs!"

"The swamp rat knows ever'thin!"

And off they went, to spread their news.

Ossie and his family watched the sky turn bottomless blue and they heard the sun set. The swamp was nothing but water and plant and life, shimmering below them, one end to the other. A steady wind blew across the new sawgrass and onto them. The wind was warm, full of possibility, and it was in that moment that Ossie understood a thing. He understood that he was exactly where he wanted to be, with Emma, their children, here, now, the world laid out before them.

It was just as they'd been telling him, all along. Somehow, they'd known it would happen and they were right. Ossie, at last, had found his way. And it led him here.

"Lookit all the water," said the little boy rat, "just sittin there."

"Look a little closer, Hitch," Emma told him. "It doesn't sit, not really."

The boy looked. The girl looked, too. She saw and understood.

"The swamp is a river of water, wide and pure," Ossie said. "Even as we move through, it's movin around us, over us, under us. It's always movin. It never stops."

There. That is it. That is the story I set out to tell. I will let it finish here.

I have told it all, as much as I know it. Every part, exactly as it happened. Every bit, just as it was. The rest I made up, as best I could.

But in the end, it's all true. I'm almost certain of that.

As goes the Gator, so the Swamp goes